"I realized that you were the perfect match for my requirements," Bastian fielded with characteristic cool. **"However if you don't want to do it, return the fee and we'll say no more about it."**

Bastian strolled forward, lean, darkly handsome features infuriatingly calm and assured. He was disturbingly graceful in motion, not a visible ounce of tension in his big powerful frame as he stepped unexpectedly into her space.

"What on earth do you think you're doing?" Emmie gasped, overpowered by his proximity and totally disconcerted by his behavior.

"Maybe I wanted to see what I was paying for," Bastian said succinctly, indifferent to whether or not he caused offense. After all, wasn't he hiring her to do a job?

"You haven't bought me...you *can't* buy what isn't for sale!" Emmie flung back at him in fierce rejection.

"Yet I've still managed to buy your time for the whole of one weekend."

Dear Reader,

We have exciting news! As I'm sure you've noticed, the Harlequin Presents books you know and love have a brand-new look, starting this month. They look *sensational!* Don't you agree?

But don't worry—nothing else about the Presents books has changed. You'll still find eight unforgettable love stories every month, with alpha heroes, empowered heroines and stunning international destinations all topped with passion and a sensual attraction that burns as brightly as ever.

Don't miss any of this month's exciting reads:

Lynne Graham's *The Billionaire's Trophy*
Kate Hewitt's *An Inheritance of Shame*
Lucy Monroe's *Prince of Secrets*
Caitlin Crews, *A Royal Without Rules*
Annie West, *Imprisoned by a Vow*
Cathy Williams, *A Deal with Di Capua*
Michelle Conder, *Duty at What Cost?*
Michelle Smart, *The Rings That Bind*

I hope you're as pleased with our new look as we are. Drop by www.Harlequin.com to let us know what you think.

Joanne Grant
Senior Editor
Harlequin Presents

Lynne Graham

THE BILLIONAIRE'S TROPHY

A *Bride for a* **BILLIONAIRE**

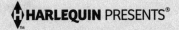

HARLEQUIN PRESENTS®

Recycling programs
for this product may
not exist in your area.

ISBN-13: 978-0-373-13167-9

THE BILLIONAIRE'S TROPHY

Copyright © 2013 by Lynne Graham

All rights reserved. Except for use in any review, the reproduction or
utilization of this work in whole or in part in any form by any electronic,
mechanical or other means, now known or hereafter invented, including
xerography, photocopying and recording, or in any information storage
or retrieval system, is forbidden without the written permission of the
publisher, Harlequin Enterprises Limited, 225 Duncan Mill Road,
Don Mills, Ontario M3B 3K9, Canada.

This is a work of fiction. Names, characters, places and incidents are
either the product of the author's imagination or are used fictitiously,
and any resemblance to actual persons, living or dead, business
establishments, events or locales is entirely coincidental.

This edition published by arrangement with Harlequin Books S.A.

For questions and comments about the quality of this book,
please contact us at CustomerService@Harlequin.com.

® and ™ are trademarks of Harlequin Enterprises Limited or its
corporate affiliates. Trademarks indicated with ® are registered in the
United States Patent and Trademark Office, the Canadian Trade Marks
Office and in other countries.

Printed in U.S.A.

H HARLEQUIN®
™ www.Harlequin.com

A Bride for a
BILLIONAIRE

The men who have everything finally meet their match!

The Marshall sisters have carved their own way in the world for as long as they can remember. So if some arrogant billionaire thinks he can sweep in and whisk them off their stilettos, he's got another think coming!

It will take more than a private jet and a wallet full of cash to win over these feisty, determined women.
Luckily these men enjoy a challenge and have more than their bank accounts going for them!

Read Kat Marshall's story in
A Rich Man's Whim
May 2013

And Sapphires Marshall's story in
The Sheikh's Prize
June 2013

This month read
Emerald Marshall's story in
The Billionaire's Trophy

Next month read
Topaz Marshall's story in
Challenging Dante

Other titles by Lynne Graham available in ebook:

THE SHEIKH'S PRIZE *(A Bride for a Billionaire)*
A RICH MAN'S WHIM *(A Bride for a Billionaire)*
A RING TO SECURE HIS HEIR
UNLOCKING HER INNOCENCE

CHAPTER ONE

SEBASTIANO CHRISTOU, KNOWN as Bastian to his many friends and acquaintances, studied the huge emerald ring in his hand with seething frustration blazing in his dark golden eyes, his lean darkly handsome features settling into forbidding lines of hauteur. He was holding the Christou betrothal ring, which had, until very recently, adorned the hand of his intended wife, Lilah Siannas.

Ironically, Lilah had not voiced a single word of reproach concerning the terms of the pre-nup agreement presented to her lawyer. Instead, while leaving the pre-nup unsigned, Lilah had become irritatingly unavailable and distant but her burning resentment had ultimately triumphed, culminating in her public statement that the engagement was over and the wedding cancelled. And ever since then Lilah had been noisily painting the town red in the company of a good-looking toyboy millionaire.

Bastian was well aware that Lilah was throwing down a gauntlet she expected him to pick up. He was supposed to be jealous: yet he was not. He was supposed to feel foolish: but he did not. He was supposed to want her so much that he would forget about the pre-nup: only he did not. No, Lilah was playing a losing game for Bastian would never marry a woman without first securing his wealth with a pre-nup agreement. That was a lesson learned well at his grandfather's knee.

His father had married four times and his three incredibly expensive divorces had decimated the Christou family fortune. Bastian's grandfather had taught his grandson that love was unnecessary in a successful marriage and that shared goals and principles were more important. Bastian had never been in love but he had often been in lust. Lilah, a tiny exquisite brunette, had excited his need to chase and possess but he had never kidded himself that he loved her. Indeed before he proposed, he had evaluated Lilah's worth much as though she were an investment. He had recognised the advantage of their similar backgrounds; he had admired her unemotional outlook, excellent education and her skills as a society hostess. But, as he now grimly reminded himself, he had seriously underestimated the strength and pulling power of his fiancée's avarice.

Bastian thrust the ring back in its case and put it in the safe, angry at the months he had wasted on Lilah, a woman demonstrably unfit to be his wife. He was thirty years old, more than ready to marry and have a family, bored with casual affairs. He had not realised that finding a wife would be such a challenge and he was already wondering how the hell he was supposed to avoid a scene at his sister, Nessa's wedding in two weeks' time because Lilah was one of Nessa's bridesmaids. Lilah would be outraged when Bastian didn't, at least, *try* to win her back. She would relish being the focus of all eyes at the wedding and would delight even more in a confrontation, but Bastian did not want his baby sister to be embarrassed or upset on her special day. The only way of avoiding that danger would be for him to arrive with another woman on his arm, for Lilah was too proud to overlook such a statement.

But at this late stage where on earth would he find another woman to act as his partner throughout a weekend of family festivities? A woman who wouldn't try to trap him into a relationship and who wouldn't read more than he meant into his invitation? A woman nonetheless capable of pretending to be intimately involved with him, for nothing less would keep Lilah at a distance. Did such a perfect woman exist?

'Bastian…?' He spun round as one of his directors strode in with a laptop beneath his arm. 'I've got something amusing to show you—are you in the mood?'

Bastian was not in the mood but Guy Babington was a good friend and he forced a smile to his hard mouth. 'Always,' he encouraged.

Guy opened the laptop on the desk and spun it round to display the screen to Bastian. 'There…recognise her?'

Bastian studied the photo of a stunning blonde with

bright blue eyes in a party dress. She was laughing into the camera. 'No...should I?'

'Take another look,' Guy urged. 'Believe it or not, she works for you.'

'No way...I would've noticed her,' Bastian instantly declared because she was such a beauty. 'What's her picture doing on the Internet? Are you on Facebook?'

Amused, Guy shook his head. 'I'm on a website advertising a business called Exclusive Companions. It's an escort agency for professionals, *very* exclusive,' he said, rolling his eyes suggestively.

Bastian frowned, his sensual mouth curling a little with distaste. 'Do you use escorts?'

'I wouldn't mind using this blonde,' Guy confided, ducking the question with a lascivious look.

Bastian elevated an ebony brow. 'You said she worked for me—'

'She does—as an intern on a three-month placement on this floor. Emmie...she does research for your PA.'

Astonishment gripped Bastian as he turned his attention back to the screen. '*That's* Emmie?' he queried in disbelief, mentally flicking up an image of the young woman as she looked at work: hair tied back, specs anchored on her nose, dowdy clothes. Still frowning, Bastian zeroed his attention in on the dark mole on the centre of the blonde's cheek as he recalled that the intern had the same beauty mark in the identical place. '*Diavelos*...that *is* her! She's actually moonlighting as an escort?'

'Evidently...but what I'd really like to know is why

she dresses to look like the ugly duckling when she comes into work here,' Guy confided.

'Her name is Emerald according to the site...'

Sebastiano flipped open his own computer and hit several buttons to access the list of his staff. Yes, it wasn't Emmie short for Emily or Emma as most people would assume; her true name was indeed Emerald. So, weird and unbelievable as it seemed to him, it *was* the same woman.

'Doesn't she clean up amazingly well?' Guy chuckled lecherously.

Bastian would not have described the intern as an ugly duckling although he had to admit that on the few occasions she had been around him she had thoroughly irritated him.

'Sugar is bad for your teeth,' she had told him when she handed him his coffee, strong and sweet the way he liked it.

'Manners maketh man,' she had quipped when he strode through a door ahead of her and they almost collided in the doorway.

But he had noticed that, even clad in the ubiquitous black tights, she had incredibly long legs, the sort a man thought about wrapping round his waist. An escort, he ruminated thoughtfully, a woman whose company was available for hire. If she cleaned up as well as she did in that photo, she would make a very presentable piece of arm candy and, after all, it would be in her own best interests to meet his expectations. Possibly she wasn't fully aware of the terms of her temporary employment, one condition of which specified that she must do nothing to bring the company into disrepute. And working a lucrative sideline as an escort for rich men definitely didn't fit the bill of acceptability. He had never used an escort service before, nor would he have considered doing so in normal circumstances, but for this particular occasion he liked the idea of a woman he could *hire* to accompany him to his sister's wedding. He would not have to ask anyone for a favour, nor would he have to pretend an interest in a woman that he didn't feel anything for and there would be no room for misunderstandings in such an arrangement: he would pay Exclusive Companions and she would deliver the act he told her to deliver. In fact the more he thought about it, the more he liked that idea; she would be as much under his control as a robot.

Emmie swallowed back a yawn with difficulty while Bastian Christou's PA, Marie, gave her exhaustive details on the company she wanted her to research. Her hand unwittingly rubbed at her aching leg, which always bothered her when she was on her feet too much. Her right leg had been badly injured in a car crash when she was twelve and for years afterwards Emmie had been disabled, initially forced to use a wheelchair and only later recovering sufficiently to get around on crutches. Indeed, without experimental surgery she would never have walked unaided again and so grateful was she still for that surgery that she always shrugged off the occasional ache as unworthy of note or fuss.

Unfortunately, her tiredness made concentration a virtual impossibility and, not for the first time, Emmie marvelled that she had ever believed that an unpaid internship would be the perfect solution to her unemployment crisis. After months working a temporary dead-end job in the local library, Emmie had been willing to try anything to get her career out of the doldrums. She had jumped, however, from the frying pan straight into the fire. Although she had several friends working for no money to gain some experience for their all-important CVs they were all, without exception, still in receipt of parental financial support.

Emmie was rather less fortunate in that field. Although she had an excellent business degree the economic downturn meant there were few graduate jobs and the few that there were went to applicants with the skills and practical know-how that were only attainable from actual employment. After countless unsuccessful applications, Emmie had known that she needed work experience to improve her chances and she had initially been ecstatic when she got through a tough assessment centre and first won the internship at Christou Holdings, one of the most aggressive and successful software companies in London.

Never having lived in the city as an independent adult, she had not initially appreciated what a challenge it would be simply to make ends meet. And then, her estranged mother, Odette, had got in touch out of the blue and had offered Emmie her spare room and Emmie had snatched gratefully at the opportunity for cheap lodgings without which she could not have hoped to accept the job. It had not once occurred to her that Odette might have an ulterior motive in inviting her to stay. Naively, Emmie had simply been eager for the opportunity to get to know the mother she had last seen when she was twelve years old. From that age Emmie and her two siblings had been raised by her eldest sister, Kat, in the Lake District and, although she had recognised Kat's dismay when she learned of the London scheme and Emmie's plan to live with their mother, Kat had not interfered and had merely warned her sibling that Odette could be 'difficult'. Well, the word *difficult* didn't begin to cover the problems she was having, Emmie reflected heavily, hoping that she wasn't in for yet another long-running row when she got home later.

Her first unsettling discovery after moving in with Odette had been the disturbing revelation that her mother made her very comfortable living through an Internet-based escort agency. The even bigger shock that followed had been Odette's firm conviction that Emmie should join her list of escorts and earn her keep that way. When Emmie had refused and had instead taken on waitressing work five nights a week, Odette had been furious and, even though Emmie was handing over every penny of her meagre earnings to her mother, Odette was still angry and dissatisfied with her daughter.

Perhaps the most upsetting experience of all for Emmie had been the dawning awareness that her mother didn't love her, cherished no fond wish to get to know her better and certainly didn't regret having left her to her sister's care at twelve years old. That learning curve had been steep and painful and had made Emmie appreciate that she had gone to live with her mother in the hope of reviving a relationship that had only ever existed in her own imagination. Sadly, Odette was not the maternal type. Her children were simply the by-products of relationships that had gone wrong and it honestly seemed as though Odette had never managed to form an attachment to any of her daughters.

'Ah, Marie…' a familiar dark accented drawl pronounced from the doorway. 'The meeting is about to start. Emmie can take the minutes for us.'

Emmie spun round, faint colour blooming in her cheeks as she focused on Bastian Christou's tall powerful frame. The Greek entrepreneur was a popular choice for profiles in leading business publications and she had read all about him long before she came to work for him. He took a brilliant photograph but was even more eye-catching in the flesh, where his height and breadth and the gleaming luxuriance of the ruthlessly cropped black hair that framed his lean, darkly handsome features were disturbingly noticeable even in a crowd. Of course he was taller than most men, something Emmie tended to notice because she was five feet nine inches tall but he topped her by a comfortable six inches. In truth he had the charisma and looks that no woman could ignore, added to a sun-kissed complexion the shade of dulled gold and the perfectly formed features of a fallen angel. His mother, she had read, had been a famous Italian film star and he looked exactly like her, right down to the burnished dark eyes that were currently engaged in roaming over her as though she were edible and he were starving. Startled by that analogy and the intensity of his continuing appraisal, Emmie tensed and jerked her chin up while throwing him a look of frowning enquiry, for he had never looked at her in that way before. Perhaps his reaction was an illustration of the strange mood that Marie had warned her that her boss was in, doubtless fallout from the broken engagement that nobody had yet dared to mention in his presence, she reasoned uncertainly.

'Of course,' Marie responded equably. A slender, efficient brunette in her early forties, she rose from her seat to follow her boss back out of the office.

Bastian surveyed his quarry, Emmie, and wondered what her first smile would look like. He was accustomed to women smiling at him, not at all accustomed to one scowling and challenging him with her head tilted at a scornfully unimpressed angle. Yet there was something familiar about her, some quality that nagged at him, making him feel that he must have seen her or met her before somewhere. That niggling awareness irritated him, for he was well aware that she did not move in his social circles but indeed hailed from some hayseed background in the north. Unless, of course, he thought abruptly, he had previously come across her when she was acting as an escort to someone he knew... Now that was a genuine possibility, he acknowledged with distaste, wondering what on earth she was doing getting involved in such a seedy way of life at her age. Or was he being naïve? Beautiful women could reap rich rewards and an enviable lifestyle from such pursuits. Indeed if she was to meet the right rich man and marry him, she could set herself up for life.

Bastian had learned at a young age that most such women *used* their beauty like a commodity, expecting it to work for them and win them special treatment. His own mother had belonged to that group. Why should Emmie Marshall be any different? He watched her take notes during the meeting, noting the faint dark shadows circling her eyes and the translucent quality of her skin. He did not think he had ever seen skin that perfect on anyone other than a child. She propped her chin on an upturned hand, head at a slant that defined her slender neck and delicate jawline. A fine strand of corn-gold hair had escaped from her ponytail to trail across her cheekbone. He marvelled that he hadn't noticed the quality of her looks sooner. But then the loose shirts and trailing mid-length skirts she wore with the specs provided an off-putting disguise and the attention had to linger to note that soft, full pink mouth with its delicious pout and very slight hint of an overbite, and appreciate that the eyes behind the unattractive spectacles were a truly dazzling bright blue. In some astonishment, Bastian registered that he was developing a hard-on while he imagined those pillowy lips pouting just for his benefit. And for how many others had she performed that arousing trick as part of her escort duties? he asked himself grimly, squashing his arousal at source, for while he never bedded innocents he had an innate aversion to sex being traded for a price. And he already knew what *her* price was, didn't he?

'Emerald's rarely available. She's very much in demand,' the voice at the other end of the phone had informed him smoothly when he phoned the escort agency. 'I can offer you Jasmine *or*—'

'It *has* to be Emerald,' he had countered. 'She's the only one I want. I'll make it very well worth her while to choose me as a client.'

And then Bastian had negotiated, a skill at which he excelled, and he had learned once again—had he ever doubted it?—that for the right price he could have anything he wanted, including the rarely available and already fully booked Emerald currently falling asleep across the table from him. He had bought her services for the weekend and he had paid an enormous price for the privilege. It amused him that she evidently had not the slightest idea of the fact and yet he marvelled that any woman could so irresponsibly sell her time and attention to strangers, who might abuse her trust. Her curling lashes were down on her cheekbones, her slim shoulders drooping as she sank lower into her seat. He stretched out a long leg below the table, found her feet and nudged them sharply with the toe of one shoe. She jolted awake again, her wide startled blue eyes flying straight to him in dismay, her full lips parting, cheeks reddening with embarrassment. He wondered who she had entertained the night before and whether sex had figured. Nine out of ten men would expect sex for what he had paid for her services. He wondered how she would feel about that and how *he* felt about that…no, *never*, no way was he going there, he thought in disgust.

Emmie collided slap-bang-crash with smouldering dark golden eyes that reminded her of a tiger's eyes and that fast her ability to breathe vanished while a humming warmth prickled and then pulsed between her legs. Shock rippled through her in reaction to that sexual response, for it had been a long time since she had felt like that. Emmie was wary and seldom reacted to attractive men, having found them invariably vain and self-serving. She was very picky, *so* picky she had yet to choose a first lover, although she had come very close to losing her virginity at university when she fell in love. Of course that relationship had gone pear-shaped the instant Toby looked at her and said, 'I can't believe I'm going to bed with a girl the living image of Sapphire…'

Wham, that astonishing admission had hit Emmie right where it hurt, crushing her confidence *and* her faith in the love he had pledged. Being the sister of a world-famous supermodel and, even worse, her identical twin had often made Emmie feel as though she had no identity or individuality of her own. Time after time men had made her feel like an imperfect copy or stand-in for her flawless sister and the resemblance between the two women was so strong that, to sidestep that humiliating association being made, Emmie generally played down her best assets and avoided her twin's company. Now she wondered what it was about Bastian Christou that got to her. Lashes cloaking her gaze, she studied him, her heart beating very fast. Why had he looked at her like that? All right, his engagement was over and he was supposedly a free agent again, but what was he playing at? Men didn't, as a rule, see beyond the plain, unflattering clothing she wore. And his former fiancée was as different from Emmie in appearance as to be almost another species, being tiny, dark and glittery rather like a manic fairy, Emmie recalled from her one fleeting glimpse of the imperious little Greek socialite. Lifting her chin, Emmie gazed steadily back at him.

Reluctant amusement rippled through Bastian's powerful frame. She had nerve and he liked that; he liked that very much.

'In my office—five minutes,' he told her coolly, thrusting back his chair and rising to his full intimidating height.

'He must want to check the minutes. I hope you kept pace,' Marie commented. 'At one point there, I was afraid you might be falling asleep.'

Emmie winced. 'It was a possibility…' *Until your boss kicked me awake.* The awareness that Bastian Christou had noticed that she was dropping off made her want to cringe and she wondered if that was what he wanted to speak to her about. After all he had never bothered to speak to her before except in passing and he channelled any instructions through Marie.

'Is there no way you can chuck in the waitressing?' Marie enquired in an undertone.

'Sadly not, but I do have only another few weeks to go here,' Emmie pointed out, relieved she had chosen to be honest with the older woman about the fact that she was working two jobs to survive.

'I hope the long hours you're working to do this pay off,' Marie retorted wryly.

And from the tone of that remark, Emmie gathered that Marie saw little prospect of her being offered a full-time position with the company. In truth Emmie hadn't really expected the internship to lead to a permanent job but naturally she had hoped to be proven wrong in that assessment. She knew that it was much more likely that another unpaid intern would be offered the position she had vacated. Why should employers take on extra staff and pay them when they could get young eager workers for nothing?

Emmie walked into Bastian's office for the first time and glanced around, taking in the cool contemporary furnishings and artworks, the almost palpable opulence of a décor where no expense had been spared. But then Bastian Christou had no need to count the cost of anything. A genius in the field of software development and an exceptional businessman, he had single-handedly built an international company out of the best-selling program he had developed before he even left university and had become an enormously wealthy man while still very young.

'Close the door,' he told her, his deep voice setting up a vibration along her spine. He was a very masculine man and it had nothing to do with his physical size. Raw masculinity was etched in his hard bone structure, shrewd eyes and the authority and assurance with which he spoke. Although he was always perfectly groomed there was nothing metrosexual about him. One had only to see Bastian Christou with his sleeves rolled up on his strong forearms, his tie torn off and collar unbuttoned to show a slice of bronzed flesh to know that he was *all* male in a way so few men still dared to be.

Emmie pressed the door shut and turned back, a shiver of disconcerting awareness filtering through her tall, slender length as she met his keen, intelligent eyes. Beautiful eyes, she thought absently, as arrestingly bright as starlight in that strong face. Her body betrayed her instantly as if, having found the chink in her armour with this one man, it had forced that tiny loophole into a dangerous crack, for her breasts stirred and swelled heavily within her bra so that it felt tight and uncomfortable. Her colour fluctuated as her nipples stung into straining peaks and suddenly she was as tongue-tied as an awkward adolescent.

'Miss Marshall,' Bastian drawled, tracking her every change of expression. 'Or may I call you Emmie?'

'Emmie's fine,' she muttered at the height of a drawn-in breath.

'Or do you prefer Emerald?'

Taken aback by that rare use of her baptismal name, Emmie hovered uncertainly. 'I don't use that name…'

'You…*don't*?' A winged ebony brow climbed as though she had surprised him and when he bent his head over the laptop on the desk, it was a relief for her to have a moment to catch her breath again while watching the light from the window behind her gleam over the glossy sheen of his luxuriant black hair.

Catching herself on that thought, she didn't know what was wrong with her and only wished she could kick her brain back into gear. Yes, he was a good-looking guy but that didn't impress her, it being her experience that handsome men were usually very aware that they were handsome and invariably offended if a woman didn't react with admiration. Not that Bastian Christou struck her as belonging to that category, she acknowledged grudgingly. She was of such minuscule importance on his scale that she was sure he couldn't care less how she reacted to him. No, it was her own self and her pride that were affronted by her breathless, nervous state in his presence. A grown woman didn't lose her ability to reason around an attractive man, at least not if she expected to be taken seriously as an employee in an executive office that was still very much a man's world.

'No, I don't use that name…never have,' Emmie proclaimed with a strained smile, recalling that he could only have got that name from her job application because she only employed it when officialdom required it. Perhaps it had lingered on his mind because it was unusual.

Bastian Christou looked up with a slight smile and inexplicably that smile of his suddenly chilled Emmie to her bone marrow. 'But that's not quite true, is it?'

Frozen there in front of his desk, Emmie blinked rapidly, unnerved by the ESP promptings that were warning her of a threat when there was no possible threat that she could see. 'Sorry?' she questioned uncertainly, having lost the thread of the conversation.

'It's untrue that you don't use the name Emerald,' Bastian declared, swivelling his laptop round for her to view what was on the screen.

Emmie's soft mouth fell wide when she saw the picture he was referring to, shock and disbelief vibrating through her from head to toe because she could not imagine how a personal photograph of hers could have ended up on the Internet for anyone to see. It had been taken at her graduation party on one of the very rare occasions when she dressed up and threw caution to the wind and the photo was still in her digital camera…or at least she had *thought* it was. 'What's this? Where did you find that photo?' she gasped strickenly.

'On the website belonging to the Exclusive Companions escort agency,' Bastian confided, noting that she had turned as white as a sheet at his admission and experiencing an entirely unexpected pang of conscience because she contrived to appear genuinely shattered by his discovery. Of course, he reasoned, that merely proved that she had the useful skill of being a good actress in a challenging situation.

'Exclusive C-Companions?' Emmie stammered, for it was her mother's business and she knew that her photograph could not have been uploaded to that website without her mother's involvement. She was absolutely appalled and stared fixedly at that colourful image with a sinking heart. How on earth could Odette do that to her? Her mother knew she wanted no involvement with her business. 'How did you find this?'

'*Not* because I was visiting the website,' Bastian asserted with dry emphasis. 'Someone else who works here drew it to my attention.'

Nausea curled in her sensitive tummy. Who else knew? How many people? Inwardly she cringed in embarrassment. Who else was now convinced that she worked as an escort outside office hours? My goodness, was everyone she worked with talking about this behind her back? Humiliation clawed at her and she cursed the day she had moved in with her mother. What on earth was her picture doing on the website when she didn't work as an escort? But who on earth would *ever* believe that now?

'It is you, isn't it?' Bastian Christou pressed.

In silence, Emmie gritted her teeth and nodded agreement, unable to see how she could lie on that score. 'But it's not what you think—'

'Allow me to know what to think,' Bastian Christou murmured, smooth as glass.

'It's none of your business!' Emmie told him, her mortification yielding to a sudden rush of resentment.

'I'm afraid it is my business,' Bastian countered levelly. 'Your employment contract with this company states that you're not allowed to do anything which might bring the company into disrepute and I'm afraid that advertising yourself on the Internet as an escort would fall within that category.'

Emmie lost colour. She could not believe that a foolish action of her mother's might have put her job at risk, but she could also understand that it was an association that any employer might consider distasteful and suspect. 'I'll deal with it,' she said flatly, her full lips compressing with determination.

'*How* will you deal with it?' Bastian asked, glittering dark eyes pinned to her with growing curiosity, his attention lingering on that soft full mouth. He wanted to rip off the spectacles and tug her hair out of that ugly ponytail and see her beauty as nature had intended it to be seen: that mane of golden hair, clear, flawless skin and glorious eyes. When most women went to great lengths to look the best they could, why the hell did she hide her beauty as though it were something to be ashamed of? And then unveil that beauty to be an escort? Had she been afraid from the start that someone in the office might recognise that photo and realise she was leading a double life? It was the only explanation he could see that made sense of such a disguise.

'I'll have the photo taken down from the website. It

shouldn't be there,' she declared defensively. 'I don't actually work as an escort—'

'But clearly you have a connection to the agency,' Bastian pointed out, amused by her vehemence, her eagerness to persuade him that he had somehow mis-understood. She had little hope of getting far with that objective when he had so recently booked and paid for her services, he conceded grimly.

Emmie squirmed, determined not to admit the de-grading truth that her connection to the escort agency was through her mother. 'I promise you that I'll deal with it and that photo will be taken down as soon as I can get it organised.'

'If you're tied into an employment contract with the agency it won't be that simple a matter,' Bastian warned her and he pushed a business card across the desk towards her. 'Feel free to contact this lawyer if you need advice or assistance on that score.'

'There *is* no contract. I told you...I don't work as an escort,' Emmie repeated doggedly, her colour high because she knew he didn't believe her and she didn't really blame him for that when her photo was on the website for all to see. She was mortified by the entire conversation but surprised that he was offering her a legal contact who could help her cut ties that didn't actually exist. Fortunately, the only tie Emmie had to Exclusive Companions was her blood tie to her ma-nipulative mother.

'Tell me, why isn't the HR department dealing with this?' she queried.

'I felt the issue needed to be dealt with immediately and without spreading the news round the office.'

Exerting self-control, Emmie clenched her teeth together. 'Thanks. I appreciate that,' she felt forced to say with very real gratitude.

'Take the rest of the day off to handle this business,' Bastian advised, further surprising her with his consideration. 'I'll clear it with Marie.'

Thoroughly disconcerted by that generous suggestion, Emmie stiffened, but she was very grateful for the chance to go straight home and confront her mother about what she had done as it was scarcely something she could ignore.

'A stitch in time saves nine,' Emmie muttered shakily, taut with rage and embarrassment and frustration that she could not clear her own name but, on another level, very grateful to have discovered that her face was on that website, so that she could demand it be removed forthwith.

Bastian elevated a satiric brow. 'Another one of your funny little homilies?'

'I was talking to myself,' Emmie breathed curtly, flushing slightly because she had picked up the habit of uttering proverbs when she was a child and tended to blurt them out mindlessly when she was nervous or apprehensive.

So far, so good, Bastian reflected cynically when she had left his office, having reacted exactly as he had expected her to and engaged in a frantic cover-up. Even so, she would get that photo down from the site and cut her ties to the agency, which would perfectly suit his requirements. He had no desire for anyone to discover that he was keeping company with an escort and once she was removed from the site there would be less risk of that happening.

CHAPTER TWO

ODETTE WAS USING her laptop in her elegant lounge when Emmie entered the apartment. Her mother was a tall woman in her fifties with the same classic blonde looks that had raised Saffy, Emmie's twin sister, to supermodel status and universal acclaim.

'My word, you're home early...did the old office sweatshop burn down?' the older woman commented flippantly.

Emmie's face was already flushed by the speed with which she had walked from the bus but now her slender hands clenched as anger rose inside her. 'You put my photo on your website without my permission,' she accused.

Impervious to her daughter's tension, Odette lifted and dropped a slim shoulder, her unconcern patent. 'Photos of very beautiful girls improve business. Lots of my clients have phoned asking specially for you and I simply say you're already booked—but if you weren't so stubborn, you *could* be making a fortune.'

'You must have taken that photo from my camera.'

Emmie was disconcerted by her mother's lack of re-action to her accusation.

Odette's blue eyes, so like her daughter's, were cold as a winter sky. 'Yes. I can't see why that should be a problem—'

'You...*can't*? But you know that I don't want any involvement in your business—'

'Although you're quite happy to live off my earn-ings from running an escort agency!' Odette sliced back with stinging effect.

Emmie reddened. 'That's not true. I'm not living off you. I give you everything I earn from waitressing—'

Odette lifted a scornful brow. 'Which amounts to peanuts!' she exclaimed. 'If I rented out that room, I could be making three times as much for it. Instead I decided to be generous and help you out with your ca-reer. Is this all the thanks I get for it?'

Emmie hovered uncomfortably. 'You know I'm grateful, but I still want that photo taken down from the site. I'm not an escort and I don't want people think-ing that I am—'

Odette settled resentful blue eyes on her. 'My girls aren't prostitutes. I've told you that before. They are companions, *professional* companions, guaranteed to be presentable and pleasant. Sex isn't included in the package.'

'As far as you know,' Emmie added jerkily. 'You don't know how your escorts behave if a man asks for something more and is willing to pay for it—'

Odette rose gracefully upright. 'No, I don't,' she

conceded. 'I'm not their keeper or their mother,' she said. 'I'm only the manager who takes the bookings and runs credit and character checks on the clients. Why are you so prudish and suspicious of my business, Emmie? The girls on my books are educated middle-class young women, who want to make a decent income. Some of them are paying their way through college…'

'I'm not condemning their choices, I'm only saying that it's not a choice I would make,' Emmie declared, lifting her head high and wondering why she was feeling so guilty and ungrateful. 'Will you take down that photo right now, please?'

'You're making such a fuss about nothing,' Odette complained. 'You wouldn't think twice about posting that photo on one of those social networking sites you use—'

'That's different. You must take that photo down and remove any mention of me from the site,' Emmie reiterated. 'Whether you accept it or not, being associated with an escort site is damaging to my reputation, and have you even thought about what it could do to Saffy's reputation? The embarrassment this could cause her?'

'What the heck has Saffy got to do with this?' her mother demanded tartly.

'My face is *her* face, or have you forgotten that we're identical twins?' Emmie retorted impatiently, wishing the older woman would stop trying to play dumb when she was as wily as a box of ferrets. 'Saffy would go spare about this if she found out—'

Odette was unmoved. 'And why should that bother you? She's already made a fortune out of her face and body. She's got a lot more wit than you have but, let's face it, according to what Topsy has told me, you and your twin are not exactly close.'

Emmie stiffened at that reference to her youngest sister, who had taken to occasionally visiting their mother and had no doubt innocently let slip personal details that Odette would happily use against her daughters if it suited her to do so. 'Saffy and I may not be close but I wouldn't do anything to harm her or her career,' she proffered tautly. 'And I certainly wouldn't want to embarrass her the way I was embarrassed when someone showed me my photo on your website today. I'm really upset about this—please tell me you'll take the photo down now...'

Odette expelled her breath on an irritable hiss, her annoyance palpable. 'I will—if it really means that much to you—'

'It does. Thank you,' Emmie pronounced stiltedly, realising in frustration that she had said nothing that she intended to say and that once again Odette had contrived to talk her down and act as the victim rather than the perpetrator. Her mother had not even apologised for stealing that photo and using it on her website, she reflected in frustration as she walked towards her bedroom to get changed for her shift at the café where she worked weeknights. But then, another voice reminded her grimly, she could not really afford to have a no-holds-barred row with her mother while Odette was allowing her to occupy her spare room. Accepting favours always came with a price.

'Unfortunately, it's no longer quite as simple as that,' Odette remarked softly.

Emmie spun round in confusion. 'What are you talking about?'

'I've already taken a booking for you—'

Emmie was stunned into momentary silence. 'How can you have taken a booking for me when I don't work as an escort for you?' she asked drily.

'The client offered me so much money, I agreed,' her mother admitted without shame or embarrassment. 'I need the money and, let's be frank, so do you.'

'Well, you're just going to have to give the money right back again!' Emmie shot back at her mother in angry disbelief. 'I'm not for hire!'

'He's a businessman. He sent a contract over by courier and I signed it on your behalf—'

'But that can't be legally binding when I don't work for you!' Emmie protested.

'How are you going to prove that you don't work for me when your profile is on the website?' Odette enquired dulcetly.

At that suggestion of outright blackmail, Emmie went rigid. 'It's nothing to do with me. Return his money—'

Odette pushed her laptop aside and stood up. 'It's not that simple. I had outstanding bills and I've paid them. There's still a healthy cut of that money set aside for you—'

'I don't want it!' Emmie flung back at her furiously. 'I'm not going to be forced into acting as an escort so that you can make money out of me… It's not going to happen!'

'But I have no way of paying the money back,' her mother declared.

'That's not my problem,' Emmie stated curtly. 'Although I had no idea you had financial problems—'

'It's a tough world out there and an escort is a luxury. This guy's young, rich and handsome, so you can't complain on that score,' Odette told her with derision.

'I don't care…I'm not doing it, not for you, not for anyone!'

'Let me tell you just how much he was willing to pay to take you abroad for a weekend,' Odette urged thinly and she mentioned a figure of thousands of pounds that shocked Emmie rigid, for there was a much greater sum of money involved than she could ever have imagined.

'Odette…' Emmie said shakily. 'It doesn't matter what he paid you or what you signed. You can't sell me or my time like a product. I'm not for sale, and after the number of arguments we've had on this subject, I can't believe that you went ahead and accepted a booking for me knowing how I felt about the idea.'

The older woman settled icy blue eyes on her defiant daughter. 'You owe me, Emmie, and I intend to collect.'

'How do I owe you?' Emmie prompted painfully. 'You never bothered with me from the age of twelve. You never visited or wrote or phoned or even paid towards my upkeep—'

'I had a hard time surviving. And you were all quite happy living with your sister, Kat,' Odette argued tautly. 'But when it *really* mattered, I was still there for you—'

Emmie's facial muscles were locked tight with self-discipline. 'And when was that?'

'When you needed surgery for your damaged leg. When you were desperate to walk again, I came through for you,' her mother declared impressively.

Emmie was knocked sideways by that announcement. 'You're saying that *you* paid for the surgery I had on my leg?' She gasped in shock.

'Where did you think Kat got the money from?' her mother enquired drily.

Emmie was too distraught at what she had been told to continue reasoning with her unrepentant parent. She changed for her shift at the café and went to work in a daze. Was it true that Odette had paid for her surgery? It was a supreme irony that as a teenager it had not even occurred to Emmie to wonder where her oldest sister, Kat, had got the cash to pay for Emmie's private surgery abroad. Even though Emmie was now in her twenties it had never occurred to her to ask, an oversight that now struck her as unforgivably obtuse and selfish. Emmie knew how much that surgery had meant to her at the time, how desperately she had craved the normality and the independence of no longer needing assistance in almost everything she did. She was dumbfounded by the assurance that her mother had paid to make her deepest wish come true.

While she served meals and drinks that evening, her mind was lost on another plane. Her sister, Saffy, had never overcome her guilt that she had not been injured in that same crash and she had been fiercely protective of her injured twin in the aftermath. Saffy had never understood that the continual presence of her physical perfection and glowing health had only made Emmie all the more aware of what she had lost. Emmie's teen-aged experience of infirmity had been wretched and she had often been depressed. People had continually looked away from the awkward gait caused by her dis-ability, embarrassed by her, embarrassed for her, pity-ing, avoiding her as if her brain might be as damaged as her body. At the same time Saffy, blonde, beauti-ful, sporty and gregarious, had been the most popular girl in school. Emmie hadn't resented her twin and she hadn't been jealous either, but that was when she had learned to hate the wounding comparisons that peo-ple made between the two girls, one so perfect, the other so physically flawed. Those feelings had been compounded from early childhood by Odette's resent-ful attitude to having had twins when she had only wanted one child. Even worse, Emmie had proved to be a heavy responsibility, underweight when born and often ill afterwards, a sickly child continually requir-ing extra care and attention. Emmie was always pain-fully aware that in those days Odette had found caring for her too heavy a responsibility.

Her mother was in bed when Emmie got home and although it was a relief not to have to face the older woman again Emmie was still in turmoil. Odette might once have been a neglectful parent but that costly surgery had transformed Emmie's life, not least giving her her freedom and independence back. If her mother had paid for that operation, Emmie *did* owe her a debt. But surely that didn't mean she was honour bound to perform escort duties for some stranger? Hadn't Odette said 'a weekend *abroad*'? My goodness, could such an arrangement be any more bizarre or dangerous? A *whole* weekend out of the country? He could be a white slaver and she might never be heard of again.

'I'd like to see that contract,' Emmie told her mother staunchly over breakfast, determined not to let her emotions take control of her again. She needed a solution and another argument would be counter-productive.

A couple of minutes later, Odette passed her a slim document. Emmie glanced down it and leafed to the last page to see the signature and what she saw there astonished her. *Sebastiano Christou!* How was that possible? How could Emmie's boss be the man who had booked her as an escort? The same boss who had informed her that her supposed second career as an escort ran contrary to company policy? Emmie was so enraged by the sight of that particular name that she was vaguely surprised steam didn't pump from her ears. She stuffed the contract into her bag. 'I'll handle this,' she told the older woman tautly.

Evidently having expected more of a reaction from

her, her mother said, 'Aren't you surprised by the identity of the client?'

'Should I be?'

'You do work for the guy—'

'Oh, so you're aware of that?' Emmie fielded thinly.

'Of course I am. It puts a whole new spin on office romance,' Odette remarked mockingly.

'Believe me,' Emmie declared as she stood up, 'there's nothing romantic about this situation.'

Rage was powering Emmie like adrenalin by the time she reached the office. Bastian Christou was a complete hypocrite. Unbelievably, the same guy who had paid a ridiculous sum for her services as an escort had dared to warn her that her working in such a role threatened to bring *his* company into disrepute. But at least now she knew why he had been looking at her so oddly, doubtless imagining that if she worked as an escort she was a much more sexually exciting and adventurous personality than she appeared on the surface. Well, we'll just see about that, Emmie reflected, furiously gritting her teeth together.

'Mr Christou and I discussed a private matter yesterday and I need to see him as soon as possible to update him on…er, a recent development,' Emmie informed Marie.

Her eyes carefully veiled, Bastian's PA passed no comment and swept up her phone.

'Go on ahead,' she urged then, before adding, 'Be careful, Emmie—'

'Careful?' Emmie queried, glancing back over her shoulder.

'Before Lilah, Bastian had a bad track record with women,' his PA murmured warningly.

Her face flaming at the type of development that the other woman so obviously suspected, Emmie knocked on the office door and entered. Bastian surveyed her from his stance by the window, his arrogant dark head set at a questioning angle, his brilliant eyes narrowed. Emmie dug the contract from her bag and slapped it down on the desk top in explanation.

'So, you know,' Bastian remarked evenly, not one whit perturbed by her aggressive body language.

'And now it's time for you to know that it's not on, *not* happening in this lifetime!' Emmie specified with emphatic bite. 'But what I really can't believe is that you talked of how my photo on that website could bring your company into disrepute and then you went ahead and booked me!'

'I realised that you were the perfect match for my requirements,' Bastian fielded with characteristic cool, noting that with that pink warming her cheeks and her animated expression she was glowingly alive, like a candle that had suddenly been lit for the first time. 'However, if you don't want to do it, return the fee and we'll say no more about it.'

Return the fee? Consternation at that practical suggestion filtered through Emmie's anger because she didn't have a penny in the world, indeed still had an overdraft on her bank account from her student days.

Odette had admitted to having already spent some of the money and Emmie had no way of replacing it, nor was she naïve enough to believe that she had a prayer of persuading her materialistic mother to hand over what remained of that cash. 'I can't believe that you can still look me in the eye…' she said with scorn, side-stepping the money issue.

Bastian strolled forward, lean, darkly handsome features infuriatingly calm and assured. He was disturbingly graceful in motion, not a visible ounce of tension in his big powerful frame as he stepped unexpectedly into her space and without warning whisked the spectacles off her nose to examine them. 'These are clear glass…what do you wear them for?'

'Give me those back!' Emmie snapped, fit to be tied at his cheek.

With a sardonic laugh, Bastian tossed them aside and reached instead for the clip pinning her thick hair to the back of her head.

'What on earth do you think you're doing?' Emmie gasped, overpowered by his proximity and totally disconcerted by his bold approach.

The clip went the same way as the spectacles and released the heavy golden fall of her hair round her taut shoulders. 'Maybe I wanted to see what I was paying for,' Bastian said succinctly, indifferent to whether or not he caused offence. After all, wasn't he hiring her to do a job? Why should he pussyfoot around her sensibilities?

Rampant disbelief gripped Emmie as she focused

on his devastating face, struggling to block out the hard male beauty of his bronzed features, refusing to acknowledge it when he was being so objectionable. 'How *dare* you?' she snapped furiously.

'It's the truth even if you don't like it,' Bastian countered drily, watching her dark pupils dilate in a betraying sign of sexual awareness, emphasising the incredible blue of her eyes all the more. Even up close, she was dazzling, skin luminous, eyes bright, mouth sugar-pink and luscious. Raw hunger pulsed at his groin, the kick of instant and intense arousal taking him by surprise. Yes, she was very beautiful but he was accustomed to beautiful women and repulsed by those who sought payment for their attention. Unfortunately the natural repugnance he had expected to feel around her wasn't working as the barrier he had hoped it would.

'You haven't bought me…you *can't* buy what isn't for sale!' Emmie flung back at him in fierce rejection, reacting to the maddening buzz in the atmosphere that was firing a sensation of uneasy warmth between her thighs and unnerving her.

'Yet I've still managed to buy your time for the whole of one weekend.' Bastian savoured the fact, dark eyes glittering golden as hot sunlight below level black brows.

'No…no way!'

'Then return the fee and we'll forget about the arrangement,' Bastian responded lazily again. 'I'm not in the market for an unwilling escort. In the wrong frame of mind you would be useless to me.'

Emmie backed away from him, pausing to scoop up the clip and the spectacles he had carelessly abandoned on his desk. He was forcing her to accept unwelcome facts. Of course he wanted the money back if she wasn't prepared to deliver the service he had booked and she wasn't *able* to return his wretched money to him! It put her between a rock and a hard place and frustration roared through her. Had Odette won their battle so easily? She could deny all connection to her mother's escort agency and leave Bastian Christou to pursue the return of the money he had paid, but that would undoubtedly plunge Odette into serious legal and financial trouble. And the woman who had financed the surgery that had given Emmie the opportunity to live a normal able-bodied life again deserved better than that from her, Emmie conceded reluctantly. The gift of that life-enhancing surgery truly was a debt that could never be repaid.

'Why the disguise?' Bastian enquired indolently. 'Are you afraid of being recognised in the day job?'

Emmie went pink again. 'Something like that.'

She couldn't tell him the truth, had never told anyone the truth. When Saffy's face had gone global and her twin was constantly pictured in the media, Emmie had no longer felt that her face was her own. Even more awkwardly, people had started mistaking her for Saffy in the street and it had got embarrassing: strangers approaching her asking for autographs and photos, men coming on to her, people getting angry and abusive when she insisted that she wasn't the famous Sapphire because they didn't believe her. The attention had mortified and intimidated her, making her feel like a fake copy of her famous sister, incapable of satisfying people's expectations. She had always been a very private person and could never have put herself on show as her sibling had done to make a living in front of the cameras. She had never had that kind of confidence in her face and body.

Bastian relaxed back against the side of his desk. 'If you make a good job of the role I have for you I'll pay you a bonus,' he told her smoothly. 'This is very much a business arrangement, not a pleasure trip.'

Emmie wondered if this was what he always did when a woman became difficult: offer her more money, clothes, jewellery, *whatever*? Did he often use his wealth as a bribe?

'Are you in the habit of using an escort service?' Emmie enquired flatly.

'You will be the first…and the last,' he informed her grimly.

'And why didn't you tell me what you'd done when you spoke to me yesterday about the photo on the website? Wasn't that complete hypocrisy?' she asked him drily again.

'Common sense. If I take you to my sister's wedding, I naturally don't want your escort identity to still be visible online,' he pointed out coolly. 'And I'm not a hypocrite. What you see is what you get. I'm a very forthright guy.'

'Your sister's wedding? You want me to accompany you to a family occasion?' Emmie prompted in surprise.

'I don't want anything to take the gloss off my sister, Nessa's big day,' Bastian admitted. 'Seeing me with you will persuade her that I have moved on from my broken engagement and that will make Nessa happy. She's a very soft-hearted soul. And as my ex is one of her bridesmaids, it will be more comfortable for everyone present if I have a partner of my own.'

'One of her bridesmaids?' Emmie grimaced at the concept. 'Sticky—'

'But less so with you on my arm,' he confirmed. 'May I assume that you will be accompanying me to my home in Greece?'

Emmie gulped at the prospect, thinking frantically about how she could possibly repay the fee he had paid, knowing that, short of a lottery win, she could not. There was no way out, no convenient escape route. What was one weekend to be spent in the company of family and wedding guests? It sounded innocent, *safe*. She swallowed hard and then nodded in surrender, curling lashes lowering over her angry gaze.

'All that remains is the provision of suitable clothing for you to wear over the weekend,' Bastian remarked.

'That won't be necessary—'

'It *will* be,' Bastian contradicted, derisive eyes dropping to scan her loose shirt and ill-fitting skirt. 'I'll organise a stylist and personal shopper to furnish you with what you will require. Naturally I'll cover the bills. I have your phone number. I'll text you with the details.'

Emmie swallowed hard, dislike and resentment combining in a tangled knot of defiance inside her. He was treating her like an inanimate object to be correctly packaged for public show. He saw her as an escort, a woman for hire and, even though she told herself that she was doing this for her mother's benefit and to repay a debt, it was an utterly humiliating process and not an experience that she would forget in a hurry.

CHAPTER THREE

OUT OF THE corner of her eye, Emmie saw heads turning as she walked through the airport. She was mentally offering up a prayer that that would be all the attention she attracted when a man with a camera stepped right into her path. 'Stop right there, Sapphire!'

Head high, face expressionless, Emmie sidestepped him, not even bothering to pause and contradict his assumption that she was her sister because she had learned that people and the paparazzi in particular refused to credit that she was not who they thought she was. After all, a photo of Sapphire was worth a lot of money and no pap ever wanted to admit that he had made a mistake. Dressed as she was in designer gear, Emmie knew there was even less chance than usual of anyone believing that she was not her twin. The mini wardrobe of new garments packed into the sleek case she was wheeling was not bargain-basement fare by anyone's standards. Indeed Emmie had never in her life worn such expensive clothing and, ironically, knowing that she looked her best had lifted her confidence.

That acknowledged, however, the prospect of a weekend at the Christou family home still had her nerves leaping about like jumping beans. There was a tight hard knot of anxiety in her abdomen as well, for nothing she had since learned about the Greek billionaire had eased her misgivings in the slightest.

Before his engagement Bastian had been a notorious womaniser and her Internet searches had offered her fertile information on his likes and dislikes for, in common with many rich, high-profile men, he had occasionally fallen victim to the kind of lover who sold her story of their intimate dealings to a newspaper for cash. There had been a sordid little tale of a chaotic affair with two sisters, more than one cringe-worthy reference to his penchant for early-morning sex and all the usual fillers about the extravagant gifts he bought, how easily he got bored, how quickly and coldly he severed ties when he lost interest. At the office he was a neat freak with everything in its place and no clutter and definitely on the emotionally detached side of sociable. Emmie had learned nothing else worthy of note and very little about his true nature. He was extremely intelligent but, having studied his career, she had already known that for a fact. He had built his business from the ground up and it had soared to meteoric heights.

Bastian saw Emmie walking towards him and experienced a rare instant of shock. She was a vision of golden loveliness and sophisticated elegance in tailored cropped trousers, sky-high heels and a soft clingy top. He tensed. Perfect for the role, he told himself sharply;

nobody would doubt the veracity of his relationship with a woman who resembled a screen goddess with her simply amazing face, long lazy walk and incredibly shapely legs. OK, shorn of disguise and in the right clothing, Emmie Marshall was absolutely gorgeous, but he was *not* personally affected, he assured himself on the back of the reminder that he had always preferred small, curvy brunettes. But the cut of his trousers still felt too neat and his strong jawline clenched hard. A little reaction was normal, he conceded grudgingly. He would be dead from the neck down if he didn't react to Emmie at all and didn't wonder if that luscious pink-tinted mouth would taste as good as it looked. Only at the last possible moment did he finally appreciate that she was being pursued by a couple of men waving cameras and he could not work out why he had not noticed them first. He signalled his bodyguards to protect her from the intrusion.

'Emmie…' he breathed.

'Mr Christou,' Emmie replied glacially, resisting with all her might the sheer raw charisma of Sebastiano Christou, sheathed in a dark designer suit perfectly tailored to his lean powerful frame, his jawline darkened by faint stubble, heavily lidded dark golden eyes fringed by amazing black lashes resting on her like a gun to a target. Bull's eye, she thought maniacally, a burst of heat warming her pelvis, breasts high and taut, her entire body positively leaping into a terrifying state of electrically charged sexual awareness.

'Bastian…' he traded drily a split second before he reached for her.

Emmie was so startled by the manoeuvre that she froze like a rabbit in headlights. She had convinced herself that she had nothing to worry about with Bastian Christou. After all, he wasn't going to be getting much time alone with her at a big family wedding. Not only was she not his type, being blonde and about a foot too tall, but he also only wanted her on his arm for show. And then he kissed her and her every conviction that she was safe fell at the first hurdle.

He caressed the corner of her mouth with his firm male lips and she tingled all over, every sense awakening. Her lips parted and then he surged in like an invasion force and took shameless advantage. It was an explosive kiss and she was lost in it as unfamiliar excitement blasted through her slender body with every delving dart of his skilful tongue. It was agonisingly intimate, much more so than any kiss had ever been for her. Little tremors of shocked reaction quivered through her, the inner burn at her core exercising an almost unbearable ache as he set her back from him with strong hands, eyes so dark they glittered like polished jet in his hard face. Her legs felt dislocated from the rest of her body and that ache, that ache she dimly recognised as unfulfilled desire, clawed cruelly at her. For a split second she wanted to snatch him back into her arms and conduct a wild experiment on him. It didn't matter that he was her boss or that they were in a public place. All that was driving her in that moment was a fierce need to feel that same wild conscience-free excitement again and see where it would take her.

'I wasn't expecting actual ph-physical contact,' Emmie told him shakily while in the background a man with a camera argued volubly with one of Bastian's security men.

'You can't be that naïve. We're supposed to be lovers. Anyway, what's a kiss worth?' Bastian derided with an elegant shrug of dismissal.

On her terms it had been more than a kiss; it had been the kind of intoxication she felt as if she had been waiting for all her life. But that was a silly immature thought more worthy of a teenage fantasist than a grown-up, she scolded herself, fighting to stay cool and in control. A kiss was just a kiss: he was right. And that he should know how to do it so well was hardly surprising with his reputation. Even less surprising was that she should finally lust after a man in earnest. It was only proof that she was a normal breathing woman, nothing she needed to agonise about…at least as long as she didn't surrender to the temptation.

Bastian was still seething with himself as they boarded his private jet, hostile eyes veiled, jawline clenched, handsome mouth compressed. *Diavelos*, she was a freaking escort, admittedly not a hooker, but he remained deeply suspicious as to exactly what following such a profession entailed. Obviously pleasing men went hand in hand with the role, so was it really a revelation that she turned him on hard and fast? No, to cope with such a job she had to be a practised flirt and seductress and confident she could handle a man. Well, there was no way that she was going to get the chance to handle him! He had principles, standards and hell would freeze over before he went to bed with a hired escort!

Listening to Bastian growl at the steward's efforts to ensure his comfort, Emmie rolled her eyes and picked up a magazine. He was in a bad mood and he wasn't polite enough to keep it to himself. Those lustrous eyes below those thick sooty lashes were positively smouldering, his spectacular bone structure set like granite below his bronzed skin. Why? He was the one who had launched the kissing thing. Men! Who needed them? Odette always had, she reflected unhappily.

Emmie had few happy memories of her childhood years with her mother. Odette had divorced her father when he went bankrupt. It had been a very bitter divorce and when the twins' father had remarried and begun a second family, he had immediately decided to forget that he already had two children. Emmie had last seen her father when she was twelve years old. She knew where he lived, knew what his wife looked like and the names of her half siblings: that was the joy of the Internet, which enabled spying from afar and which had satisfied her curiosity. With her sister, Kat's encouragement she had written to her father when she was a teenager requesting contact but he had never bothered to respond, his silence making his lack of interest clear. His detachment teamed with her mother's lack of affection had hurt deeply.

While she was still getting work as a model, Odette had enjoyed a never-ending stream of men in her life and she had brought every one of those men home. The only one who had even been passably nice and semi-interested in Odette's daughters had been the father of Emmie's youngest sister, Topsy, a South American polo player, whose affair with her mother had died a natural death when he went home again.

Emmie had sworn that she would never *need* a man in her life. Men were demanding and difficult; men took over; men were *selfish*. She watched Bastian help himself to a drink from the built-in bar without offering her anything and suppressed a sigh: he was putting out enough moody bad-tempered vibes to cast a claustrophobic storm cloud inside the spacious cabin.

'You sulk like a girl… Do you throw a tantrum afterwards as well?' Emmie heard herself say without even thinking about what she was saying. But she was fed up, *really* fed up. Here she was dressed up exactly as he had requested, punctual, smiling…well, not perhaps smiling, she conceded reluctantly, but at least she was willing to *try*, which was more than he was.

In astonishment, Bastian swung round and settled outraged golden eyes on her in disbelief. 'What did you say?'

'You're very temperamental and I'm doing the best I can but I suppose I shouldn't have used those particular words,' Emmie responded ruefully. 'If it wouldn't be too much trouble, I'd like a drink as well. A pure orange if you have it…'

The slightest tinge of colour accentuated his carved cheekbones at the unspoken reminder that he had not offered her a drink. He lifted a bottle and uncapped it.

'It's all right, you can relax,' Emmie told him with helpless amusement as he extended the glass to her. 'I already know you don't have any manners.'

'What the hell gives you the idea that you have the right to insult me?' Bastian thundered down at her.

Emmie was not intimidated. 'I didn't think it was an insult to tell you the truth. You never say please or thank you and you walk through every door first. You're a very rich and powerful man, most people you meet are subordinate to you and naturally you have learned to take advantage of that. *Might is right. Money talks.* That's how the world works, so I can't even blame you for it.'

Bastian was stunned by the level of sheer indignation rising inside him, but then he could not remember ever having been attacked in such a way by a woman before. Generally women bored him stiff with their fawning flattery. Who did she, a little office worker going nowhere, think she was to criticise *him*? And if this was 'trying to please', what did she do for an encore? Pull a gun on him?

'I do not take advantage of my employees!' Bastian shot back at her, because although he would very much have liked to say otherwise he could not recall the words 'please' and 'thank you' *ever* figuring much in his vocabulary. But then he was a man of few words, he reminded himself furiously, but he made those few words *count* and issued clear concise instructions that were rarely misunderstood. In addition, for the past two years running his company had won an award for being one of the best to work for, offering as it did unrivalled working conditions to its employees.

'Well, you certainly take advantage of Marie,' Emmie fielded without hesitation. 'I did her time sheets and I know that for a fact. I'm sure you pay her an excellent salary—'

'I do,' Bastian sliced in grittily on the score of his trusted PA, while wondering how on earth he would tolerate Emmie for an entire weekend without killing her.

'But I doubt if it's enough to warrant keeping a married mother of three working until eight at night on Christmas Eve,' Emmie tossed back. 'Or for taking her abroad to work on her fortieth birthday, so that she had to reschedule her party.'

'I didn't *ask* Marie to work late on Christmas Eve. As for her birthday, as I have no idea when her birthday is I can't comment. But I will point out that if she didn't choose to mention a prior arrangement to me, you can't blame me for it!'

'It was Christmas Eve. You told her the work was urgent and she did it,' Emmie expanded gently. 'Of course she did. She's very diligent. A considerate employer would have appreciated her position on that particular day of the year.'

Bastian ground his even white teeth together. 'Keep

quiet,' he told her harshly. 'I don't want to hear another word out of you for the remainder of the flight!'

Emmie made a teasing zip-up gesture across her lips, which went down like a lead balloon. She veiled her eyes, cloaking the amusement there and then glanced at him again. She knew she was annoying him and she didn't feel the slightest bit guilty. Well, he shouldn't have kissed her, she reasoned, still resenting that breaking down of boundaries. *That* had been a step too far in their pretence. She glanced up again, collided unwarily with burning golden eyes and felt heat surge as if he had lit a torch inside her. Her cheeks burned. Standing there, tall, lean and dark as sin, even with that brooding sardonic slant to his hard chiselled features, he was too gorgeous for words.

'You shouldn't have kissed me,' Emmie said abruptly into the heavy silence.

'And how do you expect to put on a convincing act of being my girlfriend in my home if you can't cope with one little kiss?' Bastian derided.

'There was no need for you to touch me. There were no witnesses at the airport who needed to be convinced of anything,' Emmie pointed out. 'We'll get along better if you respect the ground rules—'

'*What* ground rules?' Bastian demanded grimly.

'Please don't touch me unless you absolutely have to.' Emmie studied him with clear blue eyes and lifted her chin. 'You may have bought my time but don't make the mistake of believing you've bought anything else.'

'Are you saying that you have *never* slept with a client?' Bastian pressed with so much incredulity in his voice that she wanted to slap him hard.

'Never,' Emmie told him vehemently.

'Next you'll be telling me you're a virgin and pure as driven snow!' Bastian exclaimed, throwing his long powerful body down into a seat and flipping open his laptop with an air of purpose.

As that was exactly what she was and little opportunity had recently arisen for her to redress the condition, Emmie compressed her lips and returned her attention to the magazine she had abandoned. She had said what she *had* to say because she needed him to know upfront that sex was not an option. For an instant, she wished she could simply tell Bastian Christou the truth, but the prospect of explaining that her mother ran an escort agency and had virtually blackmailed her into accepting his booking stuck in her throat. It would be too degrading to admit that her mother would do virtually *anything* for money. After all, mud always stuck. He wouldn't believe that she had never worked as an escort before either, and that he was, in fact, her first *and* last client. Anyway, why was she worrying about what he thought of her? Why should that matter to her? Bastian Christou was simply a filthy-rich, domineering and very spoilt male and she wasn't one bit surprised that he had had to hire an escort rather than approach an obliging female friend for assistance. She wouldn't be a bit surprised to discover that he didn't *have* any female friends.

In a state of festering irritation, Bastian watched Emmie sleep, a long slender hand topped with delicate pale pink nails tucked below her cheek, luscious lips parting infinitesimally on every breath, superbly long elegant legs stretched out and crossed at the ankle— very dainty ankles too—golden hair tumbling like a waterfall of glorious silk across her sweater. For an escort, she wasn't very good on the entertainment front, he mused, his full sensual mouth compressing. Of course to be fair if she had chitter-chattered all the way from London, he would have been ready to strangle her by now, but the complete unconcern and indifference to his opinion that had allowed her to fall asleep in his company was almost an insult. If he was honest, he had expected her to flirt like mad and make a move on him, using the opportunity he had given her to get close to him. As a young, extremely rich and presentable man he was accustomed to receiving that attitude from her sex. Women tried to impress him, charm him, seduce him… They didn't just fall asleep as if he were a piece of furniture! Bastian ground his perfect teeth together again, struggling to suppress the suspicion that he was disappointed that she wasn't all over him like a rash.

Emmie slept right up until the jet landed in Athens and stumbled drowsily onto the helicopter that was to convey them the final leg of their journey to the island of Treikos. 'Your own island…I should've expected that, shouldn't I?' she mumbled abstractedly, speaking her thoughts out loud. 'Owning your own island is almost textbook Greek billionaire.'

'Treikos belongs to my grandfather, Theron,' Bastian said flatly.

'I take it…your mood hasn't improved?' Emmie remarked gingerly.

'There is *nothing* wrong with my mood!' Bastian ground out, what little patience he possessed challenged beyond tolerance level.

Eyes flaming gold below sinfully long black lashes, he was moving his hands in a violent arc, suddenly for the first time striking Emmie as thoroughly foreign and exotic. He said more as well but she couldn't hear him because of the noisy ignition of the helicopter. Getting airborne again was a relief while she deliberated on the way she had been reacting to him. Her cheeks reddened on the awareness that she had taken her resentment of her position out on him when it would have been more just to take it out on her mother. She had needled Bastian, criticised him, even scorned him. Right there and then, she was shaken to have to accept that she could behave like that. She swallowed hard. He had paid a small fortune for a pleasant companion and had instead received a venomous and truculent one.

As it would have been quite impossible to communicate with him while they were airborne due to the noise level inside the helicopter, Emmie dug a pen out of her bag and wrote on the back of her hand and then extended it to him so that he could see what she had written.

When it came to women, Bastian considered himself to be incapable of surprise at anything a woman did, but when Emmie printed 'I'm sorry' on the back of her hand and thrust her apology at him, he was strongly disconcerted by her approach. He blinked, looked again and then suddenly he wanted to laugh, but he didn't want to hurt her feelings when he genuinely admired the wholehearted honesty of her admission that she had been challenging company. In answer he caught her hand in his and kissed her fingertips in forgiveness.

Equally startled, Emmie tugged her hand back, fingers tingling from that brief salutation. He had style and he really *didn't* sulk, she conceded guiltily. But it *was* partly his fault that she had been behaving badly. Good grief, that kiss had knocked her sideways and she hadn't been able to cope with that! She had believed that she had made a total fool of herself when she responded to him. She stole a sidewise glance at his bold bronzed profile. But she was undoubtedly dealing with a guy who *always* got a response out of a woman. He was downright beautiful and she could have kissed him for an hour without getting bored, stunned by the bonfire of reaction one kiss could light in her body. Even so, what she was experiencing was only sexual attraction and perhaps she had never felt it so strongly before, she reasoned, wishing she didn't want him to do it again, wishing she were back safe in his office where such temptation had been unknown and he had been a distant figure whom someone as insignificant as her rarely saw, never mind got close to.

'You were right about the manners,' Bastian admitted wryly as he helped her out of the helicopter again, his bodyguard bringing up the rear. 'I have no excuse. I spent years at an exclusive English public school where I learned every courtesy. Then I went to visit my mother in Italy one summer when I was fourteen and...er, lost the habit—'

Surprised by that far from arrogant and generous concession, Emmie turned to look at him. 'Why? What happened?'

'My mother said that every time I opened a door for her it made her feel like an old lady and that all the thank-yous I used made me sound like a waiter.'

'I know some women do believe that a man being courteous to a woman these days is sexist,' Emmie allowed, resisting a strong urge to criticise his parent. 'But I don't think that way.'

'Obviously not.' Dark eyes dancing with raw amusement, Bastian shot her a glance, making her maddeningly conscious of his thick dark eyelashes. 'I was trying so hard to impress my mother, and make her proud of me because I didn't see her very often, but evidently I overdid it.'

Or his mother was an unfeeling shrew, Emmie reflected in pained silence, in much the same way as Emmie had been to judge Bastian on appearances and assume that his wealth and status explained his seeming lack of manners.

'I suppose I was sort of prejudiced about you,' Emmie admitted ruefully.

'Ditto,' Bastian added.

'I'll try very hard not to hold your money against you,' Emmie muttered.

Bastian almost laughed out loud, for it was the very first time it had been suggested to him that his fortune could act as a source of prejudice. 'And I will try equally hard not to cherish misconceptions about your…er, profession outside the office.'

Emmie winced. 'Don't use that word, "profession",' she advised. 'It's misleading when you think of that reference to "the oldest profession of all".'

'You're right. That wasn't tactful.'

Feeling almost in charity with him, Emmie was taken aback when he reached down and closed his hand round hers and her bright blue eyes dropped to their linked fingers in silent question.

'We're in view of the house. We now have those witnesses you said we needed before I could touch you,' he extended in calm justification.

Emmie was tense, intent on the sheer novelty value of Bastian smiling at her, even if it was fake and for public show. Good grief, it was an incredible smile that utterly transformed his face, chasing the detachment she had so often glimpsed there. Reddening, she looked ahead of her and only just managed not to gasp like an overexcited child at the sight of the huge white rambling modern house sprawling along the edge of the beach. 'That's your home?'

'I demolished my father's old house and had this one

built about six years back. Before that I stayed with my grandfather, who lives on the other side of the island…'

It was a massive house. Nervous butterflies leapt in her tummy at the thought of the family occasion she was about to crash in her false identity of girlfriend, not to mention the ex-fiancée, who she assumed would be present the night before the wedding in her role as bridesmaid.

'You know we haven't discussed any sort of cover story,' she pointed out belatedly. 'Where will·I say we met?'

'The office. Keep it simple but I doubt if you'll be asked nosy questions. As a rule my relations are afraid of offending me and should be civil and reserved,' Bastian reassured her.

That didn't exactly suggest a warm and friendly welcome to Emmie and she felt more than ever like an intruder on private territory. It wasn't possible to get more personal than seeing someone's home and family. The warmth of his hand on hers was strangely comforting in spite of the fact that it was only part of the masquerade. He had such big hands that her hand felt lost in his. She sucked in a sustaining breath.

'Stop stressing,' Bastian urged. 'You're only here to smooth over any potential unpleasantness on my sister's big day.'

That was not a comment designed to give Emmie a swollen head, she conceded with reluctant amusement. 'Won't your ex resent me being there?' she asked abruptly.

'She doesn't care enough to resent you,' Bastian drawled without expression.

'And *this* is the woman you were planning to marry?' Emmie prompted in a voice of disbelief.

'Some of us don't pin much faith on hearts and flowers.'

And then a private conversation became impossible as they climbed the steps to the front door where the housekeeper, a widely smiling older woman, was already shooting a flood of welcoming Greek to Bastian and he was replying in kind.

'They're all out by the pool,' he explained, releasing her hand to lead the way through a vast echoing hall ornamented with a sweeping staircase.

Emmie breathed in deeply, smoothing damp palms down over her trousered legs and straightening her slender back when she heard the noise of voices, splashing and the shouts of excited children. Bastian strode ahead of her out into the sunshine again and a young blonde woman leapt up with a delighted grin to call, 'Bastian! I thought you were never going to get here!'

As Bastian had momentarily forgotten her presence, Emmie hovered uncertainly by the poolside, infuriatingly conscious that she was the focus of all eyes but *his*. And then someone cannoned into her, knocking her off balance in her high heels and she went flying with a cry of fright into the pool. It happened so fast that she had no way of trying to stabilise herself and her head struck the edge of something hard and blackness claimed her.

* * *

Emmie recovered consciousness to find herself lying flat on a gigantic bed in soaking wet clothes. Pain was pulsing at the back of her head and she moaned, lifting her hand to gently trace the source of the sizeable bump beneath her hair.

'Do you feel sick?' a familiar voice asked and she lifted her swimming head and began to sit up only to find a large hand planted to her midriff to press her down flat again. 'Lie still. You gave your head a hell of a thump,' Bastian told her harshly.

'Yes…' Eyes opening, she focused dizzily on Bastian standing over her, clad only in a towel, a startling enough vision to make her stiffen. 'You're not dressed—'

'Yes, and you're dripping all over my bed,' Bastian informed her.

A sudden shiver took hold of Emmie and she registered the wet cling of her sodden garments and groaned out loud. She was still staring at the most perfect set of masculine abs she had ever seen outside a movie screen. Stripped, Bastian had the musculature of a Greek god—not a very original thought, she conceded abstractedly, considering who and what he was.

'Emmie…the doctor's coming.' Bastian bent down and scooped her up into his arms without warning. A muffled squeak of surprise escaped her. 'What are you doing?'

'I'm putting you in the bathroom so that you can

get out of your wet clothes,' Bastian told her with immense practicality. 'Do you think you can stand up?'

'I'll have to,' she muttered as he very carefully settled her down on her bare feet. 'What happened?'

'One of the teenagers rammed you and you fell in the pool. You were knocked out—'

'My word, I might have drowned,' Emmie framed shakily, her knees buckling under her. 'I'm sorry, I'm feeling dizzy—'

Bastian hauled her up against him and sat down on the side of a raised bath.

'Don't you dare try to help me take my clothes off!' Emmie warned him.

Face taut with frustration, Bastian lowered her limp body down onto the tiled floor. 'Do you really think I'm likely to touch you inappropriately in the condition you're in?' he enquired angrily.

Shivering violently with the chill of her damp clothing, Emmie rested her brow down on her raised knees. 'Just leave me…I'll be OK—'

'You really do have a very low opinion of me, don't you?' Bastian growled like an angry bear.

'Sorry,' Emmie whispered, on the edge of tears because she felt so weak while she was now also being tormented by the disastrous start she had made to her weekend with Bastian. So much for the girlfriend he wanted to use as cover! One minute inside the door she had taken a header into the pool and rendered herself unconscious and a liability.

In answer, Bastian trailed her sweater off over her

head and tossed it aside. He draped a towelling robe round her pale slight shoulders, gazing down at her while wondering why she looked so absurdly vulnerable, fluffy lashes drooping, full lower lip trembling. He didn't get involved with women who looked that breakable and had no idea what to do with her.

Emmie managed to dig her arms into the sleeves of the robe to at least cover her bra. She felt absolutely humiliated as Bastian lifted her upright again, urging her to hang onto the edge of the vanity while he freed her from her trousers with as much seductive intent as he might have used towards a cardboard cut-out. She thought of the surgical scars marring her leg and hoped he wouldn't notice them. Tears stung her eyes. 'I'm sorry about this!'

'Why are you apologising?' Bastian demanded impatiently while he struggled to behave like a man of honour and not sneak a glance at the truly spectacular female figure he had briefly unveiled. Unfortunately his own body was rather less disciplined and was already betraying him with very masculine efficiency. He cursed under his breath, wondering what it was about her that made his hormones react as if she were a rocket attack. She was destroying his self-discipline and he was well aware that experiencing desire while she was feeling wretched was the act of a selfish, unfeeling bastard. Which he was, Bastian fully accepted that, knew he was no candidate for sainthood. Of course, he wasn't going to *do* anything about the inconvenient way she made him respond with every flash of those stunning blue eyes, he reminded himself grimly. But with bleak humour he recalled how he had suspected that she might go out of her way to lure him into having sex with her. It was a suspicion that now struck him as insane. There she was hunched in the robe as though she were in the presence of a ravening beast of masculinity likely to rip it off her; no, there was nothing flirtatious or seductive about her behaviour. When had he got so big-headed that he assumed that every woman wanted him? And why was he even thinking such peculiar things?

'I gather you got me out of the pool.' Emmie guessed the reason for his lack of clothing.

'*Ne*...yes,' he confirmed in English.

Emmie walked back into the bedroom slowly and made for the bed. 'I just want to lie down for a while and then I'll get dressed and come downstairs to join you,' she promised.

'I don't think so. We'll abide by what the doctor advises when he arrives.'

Having settled back against the pillows, Emmie looked at him and turned bright red. He wasn't shy anyway. Poised in what appeared to be the doorway of another room, he had cast off the towel and was pulling on a pair of black boxers. Perhaps he didn't realise that she could see his astonishingly beautiful tawny body rippling with well-honed muscle with every fluid movement. She closed her eyes tight shut. She wanted to apologise again but knew that irritated him and sealed her lips, watching him leave, shock-ingly elegant again in a dark grey suit. Two less suited personalities than she and Bastian had never been born.

A knock sounded on the door and Emmie sat up to see a young blonde woman looking in at her. 'Do you feel well enough for a visitor?' she asked with a smile. 'I'm Bastian's sister, Nessa.'

'Of course, come in,' Emmie encouraged awkwardly, thinking that she would never have known to look at brother and sister that they were even distantly related, for Nessa was small, curvy and blonde.

'I've never seen my brother move so fast in his life as when he dived into the pool.'

'Sorry for all the fuss.' Emmie sighed ruefully. 'Who knocked into me?'

'One of my teenaged cousins. His parents are really embarrassed and they wanted to come up and apologise because it could have been a serious accident,' Nessa pointed out. 'We're very lucky that Bastian realised you'd hit your head going into the water.'

'I'm all right though. Accidents happen,' Emmie responded lightly.

'How's your head?' Nessa asked 'Do you mind if I stay a while?'

'I have a bump, that's all. Of course you can stay,' Emmie answered, charmed by Nessa's smiling friendliness.

'Are you sure you're OK?' Bastian's sister prompted worriedly, touching Emmie's hand. 'My goodness, your skin is icy cold! Get into bed and warm up. I'll get you a drink!'

Emmie scrambled below the duvet and rested her head back on the piled up pillows, very much appreciating Nessa's kind-heartedness because it made her feel less of a nuisance. 'You should be with your guests,' she said guiltily.

'Technically they're Bastian's guests because this is his house but they're all family,' Nessa told her, disappearing through one of the doors and reappearing with a glass, which she thrust into Emmie's hand. 'Drink it. I'm sure I read some place that it's good for someone in shock.'

Emmie drank and then began to cough as brandy burned the back of her throat, for she really hadn't expected to be given an alcoholic drink. The rich liquid raced like a flame though down into her chilled tummy.

'So, tell me about you and Bastian…' Nessa perched on the bed beside Emmie, bright brown eyes leaping with warmth and curiosity. 'I was over the moon when I realised he'd met someone else, and so quickly too… like magic—'

'Oh, yes, pure magic,' Emmie agreed uneasily, thinking how very young and refreshingly unspoilt Nessa seemed.

'You are so beautiful!' Nessa commented with satisfaction. 'Lilah will tear her hair out when she sees you—'

'As long as it's not mine. I don't want to upset anyone—'

'I know she's one of my bridesmaids but she's treated my brother very badly,' Nessa proclaimed, condemnation tightening her pretty face. 'He deserved better and she should have dropped out of my wedding, not insisted on carrying out her role when it's no longer appropriate.'

'Perhaps Lilah didn't want to let *you* down,' Emmie suggested, sipping at the brandy while appreciating that Bastian's sister was not at all attached to her brother's former fiancée.

'No, she wants Bastian back,' Nessa contradicted, her conviction sending a current of alarm through Emmie. 'She doesn't know my brother as well as she thinks she does though. He's tough—'

'I know.'

'He had to be tough. By the time he was eighteen years old he had lived through four divorces and three stepmothers. People don't understand what he went through and what all that did to him,' Nessa declared, fiercely defensive of her half sibling. 'My mother was the only one who didn't treat him badly.'

'That's something to be grateful for,' Emmie soothed, curious but keen to stem the flood of information, which she did not feel entitled to receive because she knew Bastian wouldn't appreciate her knowing such private stuff.

'Bastian's never had a family life. He doesn't know what one is.'

'Childhood can be challenging,' Emmie commented vaguely, touched by Nessa's innocence, comprehending why her brother was prepared to go to such lengths to ensure she wasn't upset on her wedding day.

Nessa grimaced. 'Well, I was lucky. I was spoilt rotten by my mum. But Bastian didn't have an easy time.'

'He's a very confident, *private* man,' Emmie remarked with gentle emphasis.

'That's why I'm telling you this—so that you understand him better. I mean, if you're waiting for him to tell you anything, you'll wait for ever.' Nessa pulled a comic face on the score of her brother's reticence. 'The minute I heard you worked with him I knew you would be a normal woman and that's exactly what I think he needs.'

The two women were interrupted by another knock on the door, telegraphing the arrival of the doctor with Bastian in tow.

'You don't need to stay,' Emmie informed Bastian with a stiff smile.

'I'm afraid I do. Dr Papadopoulos doesn't speak any English.'

Suppressing the suspicion that she would never ever get the last word with Bastian, Emmie nodded agreement, poker-faced. Bastian translated the doctor's questions and then Emmie's head was examined. The older man finally said that he thought that there wasn't much wrong with her that couldn't be cured by a good night's sleep. He then gave her painkillers for her headache and departed.

'I'll get up now,' Emmie told Bastian before he could leave with the doctor.

'You heard the doctor…*rest*,' Bastian spelt out grittily, noting that the mascara streaks on her cheeks suggested that she had been crying and was probably not half as composed as she would like him to believe. 'I would have been happier if he had agreed you needed to be checked out at the nearest hospital.'

'I'm OK…and this household doesn't need all that fuss the night before Nessa's wedding,' Emmie reasoned, knowing that that would carry more weight with him than any other argument.

'You could go home and try to sue me,' Bastian commented grimly.

Emmie groaned out loud. 'I'm not going to sue anyone. I'm not like that.'

His face remained impassive.

Alone again and too warm now in the robe, Emmie took it off, stripped off her damp underwear and slid back naked into the comfortable bed. A little nap would brighten her up, she told herself, but Bastian's remark, his concern that she might try to sue him for her accident, had troubled her. What sort of a life had he had and what sort of experiences that even a minor mishap taking place in his home could make him that cynical and distrustful? After all, she had suffered no lasting injury. Was he so used to being targeted by greedy people? That accustomed to those who tried to take advantage of his wealth?

CHAPTER FOUR

TWO HOURS LATER, Emmie wakened from a restful doze. Her head no longer throbbed and she felt a good deal stronger and calmer. While she slept her suitcase had arrived and she opened it up and pulled out clothes for the evening ahead. Apparently there was to be some sort of a party to which the locals were invited. She showered and washed her tangled hair, drying it carefully and renewing her make-up. The party dress was fuchsia pink with a jewelled neckline and short full skirt that swirled with every step she took in the toning shoes. She was ready for anything and prepared to be a pleasant companion, she told herself staunchly while she walked down the magnificent staircase.

In the hall below, Bastian was engaged in greeting dinner guests with his grandfather, Nessa and her bridegroom, Leonides. He frowned in surprise when he saw Emmie actually up and out of bed. And then ten seconds later, overpowered by one of the curious contradictions that continually afflicted him in her radius, he wanted to sweep her straight back between the sheets with him for company. In all his many years of freedom he had never met a woman who could hold a candle to Emmie Marshall with her golden hair bouncing on her slim shoulders, her big blue eyes bright as stars while a natural smile flashed like sunshine across her succulent pink mouth when Nessa saw her and grinned. Well, his sister certainly liked her; in fact Nessa was behaving rather as though he had got engaged again. It would do no harm to depress his sister's expectations a little after the honeymoon and mention with regret that he had moved on. As he would *have* to move on, he told himself impatiently, and stop fantasising about riding Emmie's perfect body with her legs locked round his waist, her beautiful face aglow with desire. His tall, well-built body already tense, Bastian shifted restively at the charge of unholy lust firing his every hormone to a needy flame. He had never wanted any woman as badly as he wanted Emmie at that moment.

'So, you're Emmie…' A tall white-haired elderly man greeted her with a pleasant smile and a handshake. 'I'm relieved that Bastian didn't succeed in drowning you in his pool on your first visit,' he confided. 'I'm his grandfather, Theron Christou.'

During the meal that followed, Emmie struggled to eat. Nessa had insisted that she sit beside her and Leonides while Bastian was at the head of the table next to his grandfather. Even though she was hungry she was hopelessly on edge, her fingers curving to her wine glass for something solid to hold onto because every time she glanced up she met black-fringed dark golden eyes that sent her thoughts and her speech into a complete loop even as her heart hammered and her mouth ran dry, leaving her thirsty, constantly sipping and yet still overheated. She could not control the slow burn that travelled to her feminine core every time she met Bastian's stunning eyes and, even worse, she could not suppress the sense of intense longing that constantly gripped her. This wasn't her, this was *not* the woman she was, she argued angrily with herself. She had never been the type to get over-excited by a man or whose body yearned for the touch of one. Indeed she had often thought such promptings belonged more to fantasy than reality and now all of a sudden she was finding out how naïve she had been.

After dinner, the guests moved to a large room, furnished with a buffet, a bar and a DJ where many of the islanders were already arriving with gifts and good wishes for the bridal couple. Bastian banded a guiding arm to her waist and introduced her to what seemed like dozens of people. Her head swam with names unattached to faces, and the lush scent of his cologne spiced with clean, warm male set up goose-flesh across her skin. She had never been so aware of a man, of every fluid movement of his lean, hot body, the rich timbre of his dark accented drawl above her head, the ridiculously arousing feel of the long fingers flexing against her hipbone. Her breasts were full and taut below her clothing, the tips swollen and tingling, and down below in a place she rarely thought about she was tender and embarrassingly damp. It was sheer insanity to react that way to Bastian Christou but every time she connected with his lustrous dark eyes, rational thought vanished.

Desire could make anyone stupid, she reasoned as the evening marched on with the bride and groom very much the centre of attention. Bastian was a gorgeous guy and inexperience made her vulnerable to his indescribably potent sexual charisma. Maybe she had set the bar too high before taking a lover because she had wanted to find trust, honesty and caring with one special man. Maybe if she had been a little more sophisticated she could have laughed and ignored Bastian. As it was, she was wickedly, weakly conscious of his every move, every word, every glance and it felt as if she had a bomb ticking down to detonation inside her.

'Let's dance,' Bastian breathed above her head, guiding her onto the crowded floor, and she shivered, feet hesitant to follow because she didn't want to slow dance with him, didn't want to take that risk of getting physically closer. But it was getting late and soon she would be able to retire to bed, duty done, she reckoned, as bendy and inviting as a concrete post when he tilted her hips towards his and closed his strong arms around her.

Momentarily she shivered with reaction, blindsided by the hard muscular steel of him against her softer curves, helplessly intoxicated by that sheer masculinity laced with the intimacy of his evocative scent. He tipped up her head and kissed her before she knew what he was doing, and the kiss from those firm male lips cut through her like a knife blade slashing through butter, burning and arousing wherever it touched. As her nipples constricted into stiff, straining buds a sliding sensation curled low in her pelvis, leaving her knees trembling and an inarticulate sound breaking from her throat.

Bastian lifted his proud dark head. 'I want you, *moraki mou*,' he husked.

The compelling beauty of his face at that instant inflamed her. She didn't feel like herself any more: she felt *wild*, hungry, out of control, all the things she never allowed herself to be. That thought kicked off alarm bells in the back of her head but her body and the unquenchable craving for him that she couldn't fight held her fast, pinned as close to him as his own skin. He was as turned on as she was and that knowledge was strangely soothing. The brutally hard ridge of his erection against her stomach was inescapable and shamelessly thrilling on a level she refused to think about.

'You set me on fire,' he growled almost accusingly. 'I don't do one-night stands—'

'Neither do I,' she sliced in breathlessly.

Dark eyes smouldered brilliant gold over her flushed face. 'Tonight we break the rules—'

'No…' she framed feverishly and then he kissed her again, his hard mouth stealing her protest with a passionate intensity she could not resist.

He guided her through the crush of party-goers with a word here, a wave there, smoothly ensuring that nobody intercepted them and slowed their progress. She mounted the stairs by his side, ever so slightly dizzy, lower limbs a little clumsy and, away from the music, the noise and the bright lights, suddenly conscious that she was not quite sober. How much wine had she drunk? And she had not eaten much at dinner, she recalled vaguely. Drinking on an empty tummy after that huge brandy Nessa had pressed on her—how foolish could a woman be? But the burn of that scorching kiss was still on her swollen mouth, firing an unbearable ache between her legs and destroying her self-discipline.

A lean brown hand closing round hers, he pulled her into the bedroom she had vacated earlier. His hands cradled her face, glittering dark eyes heavily lidded with desire. 'Once we get back to London *this* didn't happen. It will be our secret,' he told her arrogantly.

'It's not going to happen,' she faltered, taken aback by that ruthless assurance that warned her there would be no future beyond the next dawn. 'I'm not cheap—'

His fingertips grazed her delicate jawbone. 'You want me.'

Madly, insanely, *crazily*, she acknowledged, still fighting to think straight.

One night, Bastian was bargaining with himself, one rare night of self-indulgence that smashed his usual boundaries. *She wasn't cheap?* He had got that unsavoury message, wished he hadn't and wanted the strength of mind to evict her from his bedroom but he could no longer fight his devouring hunger for her. He pulled off his jacket with impatient hands and ripped loose his collar before he reached for her and crushed her succulent mouth below his again. Gathering her up to him, he brought her down on the bed, stretching down a hand to flip off her high heels.

His hard, demanding mouth and the plunging stab of his tongue were like a drug Emmie craved, a need as powerful and natural as taking a next breath. In a minute she promised herself that she would stop him, call a halt, assert logic, but with every demanding kiss he demolished her mental misgivings. She was flat on the bed, rejoicing in his weight, which seemed to answer some of the longing clawing at her, when he lifted her up and ran down the zip of her dress.

'Bastian…we—' *mustn't*, she intended to say but he enveloped her in the folds of her dress as he trailed it off over her head.

'We *must*,' he contradicted, second-guessing her words while burying his carnal mouth against the pulse beating raggedly at her collarbone, licking the salt from her skin with a wicked tongue, tracing a trail down to the shallow valley between her small high breasts, fingers already dealing with her bra, everything moving so fast she couldn't keep track of it or call a pause.

'I want to be sensible,' she argued frantically, spooked by the out-of-control feeling she was experiencing.

'Sensible?' he exclaimed with incredulity, straddling her prone length to rip off his shirt with positive violence, buttons flying in all directions. 'There's nothing sensible about feeling like this. Some actions are driven by instinct, *koukla mou*.'

Either instinct or appreciation kept her still, her dazed blue gaze welded to the smooth muscular planes of his magnificent brown torso. Heat hummed at the heart of her and the ache stirred again stronger than ever. Her bra was gone and she hadn't even noticed it going, was suddenly much more aware of the burn of his eyes over her bare breasts, the devastating touch of expert fingers rubbing against the unbearably swollen tips. Her spine bowed, her body reaching upward in a helpless arch as long fingers grazed down her leg and came to a sudden stop to retrace their path over the roughened stretch of skin he had detected.

'What's this?' he breathed, glancing down.

Emmie froze, more naked and vulnerable in that moment than she would have been had she wakened to find herself walking nude down a street, and she turned paper pale. 'I had surgery…years ago…there was something wrong with my leg,' she explained jerkily. 'You see, I've got some ugly scars. I'm not perfect—'

'I don't want or need perfect,' Bastian declared hungrily, running a caressing but unconcerned hand over the marks he had discovered.

'But I do want you,' he breathed thickly, eyes hot gold below sooty lashes. 'I'm as hard as a rock.'

Her pallor receded, her face burning with sudden colour as he sprang off the bed and shed his tailored trousers, the male bulge of arousal prominent in his fitted boxers. Shyness and uncertainty and apprehension engulfed her. She didn't know what to do or how to behave and yet still he was the most beautiful thing she had ever seen and she couldn't take her eyes off him. That lithe tawny body called to hers on a visceral level. Desire, she was discovering, incited much more overwhelming responses than she could ever have guessed. She had never dreamt she could want to touch a man so badly.

Bastian used his mouth to tease her rosy nipples, suckling and lingering to torment while he kneaded the full mounds of her breasts. Little involuntary sounds escaped her throat and when he ran a hand up her inner thigh she literally stopped breathing, the ache stirring again and overriding every other impulse. He raked a finger down over the tight, damp fabric of her knickers and she shuddered, intolerably conscious of the swollen damp flesh pulsing between her splayed thighs. Every reflex and hormonal reaction in her entire body seemed to be centred there.

'A woman has never made me feel this desperate,' Bastian growled in a tone of bemused disbelief as he tugged off the last barrier between them.

Emmie recognised that he was shaken up too and the fierce wanting that drove her no longer seemed quite so shameful. She stared up at him, loving the hard, angular bone structure that gave his features such charismatic strength, the smouldering eyes beneath the lush curling lashes, marvelling that mere days earlier he had still been a stranger. Nobody had ever made her feel the way he made her feel. He touched her where she frantically needed to be touched, a fingertip whispering over the bundle of nerve endings below her mound, and she jerked as if he had burned her, her entire body coming alive with electric reaction.

He snaked down her body with strong supple power and spread her thighs, and her fingers knotted into his luxuriant black hair to stop him before the first breathtaking sensation of his sensual assault engulfed her feverish body. Her teeth chattered together, shock winging through her at the ferocious intensity of her own response. He explored her with his mouth and his fingers and she twisted and arched and gasped over and over again, lost to sensation, lost to the violent need he had incited. Hungry heat spiralled in her pelvis and rose to an excruciating height and she was quivering and moaning and rising closer to the climax she sensed when he rose over her and plunged deep into her.

Pain and pleasure combined with explosive effect. Even as the involuntary ripples of orgasm clenched round his hard shaft and pulsed wildly through her she cried out in pain and he fell still, frowning down with perplexed eyes at her dismayed face.

'Don't stop!' she told him urgently, too mortified by her own cry to be willing to draw such stark attention to what she had just sacrificed. That was not something she was prepared to discuss and she dimly hoped that continuation and a more natural conclusion would stifle comment. She had not known that first time sex would hurt, suspected that she should have warned him in advance but could not imagine what words she might have employed with which to share her deepest secret.

For that reason, she squeezed her eyes tightly shut, her cheeks burning, and tried to concentrate on the extraordinary feel of him inside her as he shifted position.

'Are you all right?' Bastian asked tautly.

'Of course, I am,' she parried, for that fleeting pain had speedily receded, leaving her with only the erotic sense of his alien fullness stretching her and sinking deeper into her receptive body.

'If I was too rough, I'm sorry…you feel *amazing*,' Bastian confided with ragged emphasis, easing back with care before sinking into her again. His movement provoked a melting wave of honeyed heat in her lower body, making her heart thump fast and hard again. The excitement gathered like the eye of a storm inside her chest, every sensation intensified by his fluid rhythm.

Suddenly she was caught up in the same endeavour, fully a partner, no longer an uncertain onlooker. Her heart pounding like mad, she bucked and lifted her hips beneath him, meeting his thrusts, urging him on as the writhing electric excitement and the frenzy of need overwhelmed the last remnants of her control. She could feel herself reaching another height and she plunged over the edge with a startled cry of pleasure, quivering in the waves of ecstasy while he drove into her one last time. He vented a harsh groan of satisfaction and shuddered over her and she felt him spill inside her.

He shifted and pressed his mouth in a brief salutation to her damp brow. 'That was an unforgettable experience, *moraki mou...*'

Unforgettable for her as well, Emmie acknowledged in a daze. Even though their intimacy had begun on a note of pain he had twice brought her to a climax and she was blissfully relaxed and adrift on a fluffy cloud of well-being. She squashed the misgivings already trying to infiltrate her. She wasn't going to turn all girly and silly in the aftermath, she assured herself with determination. He had surpassed her expectations but all they had shared was their bodies, nothing more. Nobody fancied themselves in love, nobody needed to get hurt, least of all her. She was in full control of her emotions.

Bastian rolled back from her and studied her with frowning golden eyes the colour of burning amber. 'So, what's going on here?' he queried, black brows pleating. 'I don't want to misjudge you and assume that this was some bizarre set-up.'

CHAPTER FIVE

TAKEN ABACK BY Bastian's provocative statement, Emmie blinked away her drowsiness and lifted her head up off the pillow. 'A…*set-up*? Bizarre?' she repeated blankly in her confusion. 'What on earth are you talking about?'

'By all means, tell me if I'm wrong,' Bastian urged, wide sensual mouth tense. 'But I believe you were a virgin.'

Emmie sat up, hugging the sheet defensively to her breasts. Suddenly, her face was literally burning with mortification, for she had been hoping that he either hadn't noticed or hadn't guessed what had been amiss with her. 'Yes?' she gritted in a so-what tone of discouragement.

'Then why throw yourself away on me?' Bastian asked flatly. 'I'm not proud that you succeeded in enticing me into bed but I wasn't expecting anything more from you than a typical shag.'

Emmie tensed in sheer shock and anger at his accusation. 'Look, I did *not* entice you!' she snapped back.

'You're so beautiful that you've naturally been entic-ing me from the moment we met at the airport,' Bastian extended grudgingly and, recognising his pronounced discomfiture in the aftermath of his sexual satisfaction, he labelled himself a total hypocrite and sprang out of bed to distance himself from her. But he had done what he should not have done and now he had to deal with the fallout. She had proved to be a temptation he could not resist. But what he could not comprehend was that Emmie Marshall had also been a virgin. That did not make sense, nor did it match the characteristics of the adventurous and more experienced woman he had be-lieved she had to be to work as an escort.

'Believe me, it wasn't intentional!' Emmie fired back, thrusting back the bedding and snatching up the towelling robe folded over a nearby chair. She dug her arms into it and tied the sash tight, adjusting the la-pels to cover every piece of skin that she could for the last thing she now wanted to be was naked in any way around Bastian Christou. *A typical shag?* Was that all her body had meant to him? Could he possibly *be* any more insulting?

'I wasn't expecting a hired escort to be a virgin. I don't pay for sex either, I never have and never will, but I'll naturally compensate you for your...er, gener-osity—' Bastian selected the word with razor-edged care '—with diamonds and hope that they meet your expectations.'

Emmie had honestly believed that she could not feel any worse but now and without the smallest warning it was as if the bottom had fallen out of her world, leaving her hovering in sickening limbo. He truly did believe that she would want to be paid in some way for having slept with him! She was shattered and simultaneously cut to the quick by his view of her. Seemingly he saw her as barely one step removed from a hooker. A man didn't normally offer a woman diamonds in reward after sex, at least not in *her* world. And *this* was the male she had chosen to sleep with? She could only despise her blind stupidity.

In the buzzing silence, Bastian noted her pallor and the tightness of her delicate bone structure. 'Have I got this situation wrong? You did say quite plainly upfront that you weren't cheap—'

'But that didn't mean that I put a price on my body like a whore!' Emmie shot back at him wrathfully, a shudder of mortified rage writhing through her tall slender figure as she stood there, stiff with disbelief. 'I meant that I don't do casual sex, that's what I meant! I wasn't talking about money or jewels or *anything* of that nature!'

'Since I've clearly offended you, I apologise,' Bastian fielded curtly. 'But what else was I to think when you made that comment about not being cheap? You're an escort, whose company I paid for. It didn't take a fertile imagination to leap to the conclusion that you would expect some further form of remuneration for including sex in our arrangement...'

And that was the exact instant in which Emmie finally recognised what a dreadful, indefensible mistake she had made in going to bed with him, for not for one moment had he forgotten that she was an escort whose time he had purchased. Not for one moment had he truly buried his suspicions about exactly what being an escort might entail. She was the one who had forgotten the barriers between them; she was the one who had somehow crucially forgotten that he was *paying* for the role she was playing. Humiliation and regret touched her deep.

'I already told you that I wasn't an escort!' she slammed back at him fierily, golden hair tumbling round her flushed cheekbones. 'But you wouldn't believe me!'

'I saw your photo on that website. I phoned up and I booked you. If you weren't an escort, how would that be possible?' Bastian demanded drily, unimpressed, a tall commanding figure for all his state of undress.

'It's not that simple,' Emmie parried, her shoulders bowing as a wave of sudden weariness engulfed her. She sank stiffly down on the sofa by the far wall, as far as she could get from him and still be in the same room. Nothing but the unlovely truth would suffice, she registered dully. She did not have a choice: she had to tell him the truth to clear her name.

Emmie breathed in deep and lifted her head high, refusing to be apologetic about what she could not help. 'My mother owns the escort agency—'

'Your...*mother*?' Bastian said incredulously, striding into the dressing room to tug a pair of jeans and a T-shirt out of the built-in closets that lined the walls.

Her mother ran an escort agency? He was astonished and appalled by that startling piece of information.

'Yes, my mother,' Emmie confirmed between compressed lips and then went on to explain a little about her background and how her elder sister had raised her and her siblings after Odette had put her younger daughters into foster care. 'I hadn't seen Odette since I was twelve and when she rang out of the blue and said I could live with her for free while I worked unpaid for your company, I leapt at the opportunity. It wasn't just that I needed a low-cost place to live…' She hesitated and her cheeks warmed, her eyes veiling to conceal her vulnerability. 'I thought it would be a great way to finally get to know my mother as well.'

Wincing at the troubled note in her voice that she could not hide, Bastian zipped up his jeans. 'Did you know about the agency *before* you moved in with her?'

'Of course not, and the minute I did move in and she told me about it she immediately began nagging at me to work as one of her escorts,' Emmie admitted ruefully, trying not to stare as he hauled on the tee, dragging it down over his amazingly muscular bronzed abdomen. Embarrassed colour stung her face with unwelcome heat. 'She was very annoyed when I took a job as a waitress instead—'

'You work as a waitress as well?' Bastian prompted with a frown of a surprise, his attention lingering on the soft full curve of her delicious mouth, which was still swollen from his kisses. That fast he wanted her again, that fast it was a challenge to concentrate on what she was saying, and he paced restively across the room, exasperated by his overactive sex drive and yet awesomely unfamiliar with the modest art of listening to a woman talk and actually recognising her distress.

'Five nights a week. I needed the money,' Emmie pointed out reluctantly. 'But I suspect that my mother was counting on me agreeing to work as an escort for her when she asked me to move in—in fact that's probably the *only* reason she invited me to live with her in the first place. She took the photo from my camera to put it on her website. I didn't know about it. I would never have agreed to that.'

'So, if you weren't working as one of your mother's escorts, what the hell are you doing here with me?' Bastian demanded bluntly, dark eyes glittering suspiciously as he searched her pale tight face, judging her sincerity, recognising her discomfort in confiding such things about her mother. As a son who had often been embarrassed by parental behaviour, Bastian had sympathy enough with her on that score.

'I'm afraid my mother brought out the big guns to persuade me to accept the booking with you,' Emmie confided with an unamused laugh, her facial muscles locking tight with self-discipline as she broached an even more personal topic. 'You saw the scarring on my leg…'

'*Ne*…yes,' Bastian responded in Greek again, reacting to her clear discomfiture.

Emmie compressed her lips. 'When I was younger, my leg was badly injured in a car crash and I ended up in a wheelchair. Eventually I graduated from the chair on to crutches. I was disabled and if I hadn't had a private and very expensive operation abroad I would probably still be on crutches. That surgery enabled me to walk again and turned my life around. After my mother accepted your booking she told me that *she* had paid for that surgery and that I owed her.'

His face hardened. 'You didn't owe anyone anything, least of all a woman so keen to use you—and possibly your body as well—as a source of profit.'

'I felt I owed her,' Emmie contradicted with quiet dignity. 'That operation meant so much to me. It gave me normality back. When my mother admitted that she was short of money I was willing to be an escort for one weekend for her out of gratitude.'

'Therefore, you've genuinely never worked as an escort before,' Bastian breathed harshly, events finally falling into place and comprehension with it. 'But why did she keep that photo of you on her website?'

'She thought it brought in more business and when her clients asked for me, she simply said I was fully booked,' Emmie advanced heavily.

'*Ne*…yes. She tried that gambit with me until I offered her so much money she was ready to blackmail you into providing the service for my benefit,' Bastian told her with palpable distaste. 'Why didn't you tell me all this from the start? I would never have got mixed up in this nonsense!'

Emmie tensed and stood up. 'I couldn't get the

money back off Odette so what would have been the
point?'

'I'm not a complete bastard,' Bastian retorted in a
raw driven undertone.

Emmie disagreed but said nothing. *A typical shag*,
words for ever etched on her soul to shame and hurt.
No, she wasn't so brave and unafraid now, was she?
Being forced to confront the image Bastian had of her
was the most humiliating experience of her life. That
she had impulsively leapt into bed with him and sur-
rendered her virginity was something she was convinced she would regret until the day she died. Now,
she badly wanted privacy. She had said what she had
to say and had nothing else to add.

'This is your bedroom, isn't it?' Emmie guessed,
pushing a heavy hand through her hair. 'I should have
realised earlier when you got dressed here but after I
bashed my head I wasn't really thinking clearly. Tell
me, did you ever plan to respect the ground rules of
being with an escort? How could you think it was OK
in these circumstances to expect me to share a room
and a bed with you?'

Face grim, Bastian strode across the room and flung
another door wide. 'Make yourself at home in there,'
he urged.

Emmie wasted no time in picking up her suitcase,
which was spilling garments, in both arms and stalk-
ing through the door. She walked back and entered the
bathroom to remove her toiletries, ignoring the spill of
her clothing beside the bed. There was just no way she

could pick up her knickers without feeling demeaned, she acknowledged wretchedly, shame threatening to overwhelm her.

'What are you planning to do tomorrow?' Bastian enquired coolly.

Emmie turned her head, bright blue eyes equally cool. 'What you paid me to do. I like your sister, Nessa. I'll still act like your partner but strictly in a hands-off way.'

She closed the door, turned the key in the lock with a click and breathed again. Good grief, she *hurt*! But then what had she expected from what could only be a casual sexual encounter? Well, certainly not the level of humiliation that he had unleashed, she replied inwardly. A knock sounded on the door and she froze, lovely face paling again.

Swallowing hard, she unlocked it. Bastian handed her an armful of her clothes and she grasped them, tilting her chin in defiance, refusing to cringe.

'One more thing,' he breathed tightly. 'Are you using any form of contraception?'

Her eyes widened to their fullest extent.

'I gather that's a no?' Bastian prompted. 'Unfortunately I didn't either. I forgot—'

'You...*forgot*?' Emmie exclaimed in disbelief.

'I've been in an exclusive relationship for a long time and precautions were unnecessary,' he stated curtly. 'I had a recent health check and can confirm that I'm free of any infection but there's obviously a risk that you could conceive.'

By the end of that speech, Emmie had lost all her angry colour. She clutched her clothes tightly to her chest. 'Oh, my word…I hope not.'

'If there is a problem, be assured that you will have my full support.' His dark eyes gleamed like polished ebony below his lush lashes and her heart thumped rata-tat-tat in a tattoo below her breastbone. It shamed her that even in that instant of stark fear she could still react like a schoolgirl to his raw dark charisma. 'I don't know if it will be any consolation…but I regret what happened between us as much as you do.'

Emmie nodded, face blank, said goodnight and closed the door, not bothering to lock it again, ESP telling her that she had nothing more to fear from Bastian. So, *he* had regrets…well, bully for Mr Insensitive! *A typical shag*, not a label she would ever forget, not how she would have wanted to remember her first serious sexual experience. She sped into the en suite shower and washed herself thoroughly. There was a dulled ache between her legs and her full mouth turned down at the corners. Suck it up, she told herself angrily. She was the author of her own misfortune but surely she had been punished enough? An unplanned pregnancy would be a disaster for her. Suppressing that concern on the belief that there was no advantage to foreseeing trouble that might not happen, Emmie got into bed and lay in the darkness, tears trickling down her cheeks.

CHAPTER SIX

EMMIE NIBBLED WITHOUT appetite at a piece of toast, no criticism of the truly sumptuous breakfast that had been delivered to her in bed: she simply wasn't very hungry, and when a knock sounded on the door that led onto the corridor, she froze and paled.

'Come in!' she called, stiff as a stick of rock.

Bastian's sister, clad in a dressing gown with her up-swept bridal hairdo gleaming with pearl pins, erupted through the door, her eyes anxious. 'I can't believe you're *still* in bed, Emmie!' she exclaimed.

'Sorry, I slept in. Do you need help with anything?' Emmie asked guiltily, wondering what had happened to etch that worried look on the other young woman's face.

'Lilah arrived first thing this morning and she won't leave Bastian alone!' Nessa relayed with unconcealed resentment. 'You should be down there protecting him!'

'I think Bastian's well able to protect himself,' Emmie replied gently, but she couldn't prevent her facial muscles from tightening at the prospect of meeting Bastian's ex, the day after she herself had slept with him.

Nessa frowned and stared back at Emmie. 'Do you really not care?'

Emmie belatedly recalled the role she was supposed to be playing and registered that she wasn't acting as a concerned girlfriend might. Or at least the sort of girlfriend who let all her feelings hang out in conversation with his sister. 'I'll be downstairs as soon as I'm dressed,' she promised ruefully. 'But stop worrying. I honestly don't think he wants Lilah back.'

'I've known men as clever as my brother trapped by gold-diggers before…not least our father,' Nessa countered with surprising cynicism. 'Lilah will do and say anything to get Bastian back. She's a barracuda and he took her by surprise—she didn't expect him to just let her go when she broke off the engagement!'

Wide-eyed at that information, Emmie gazed back at Nessa. 'Is it wrong of me to admit that she sounds a bit much for me to handle?'

Nessa laughed and sighed. 'Don't let Lilah intimidate you. You're the woman Bastian brought to my wedding.'

The bride's phone buzzed and she pulled it out, muttered something about a make-up session and fled. Emmie pushed away the tray and got out of bed. It was time to do what she had been paid to do…what her mother had been paid for Emmie to do, she adjusted wryly, while recalling Bastian's attitude to what Odette had done. Maybe she should have stood her ground and ignored Odette's efforts to guilt her daughter into doing something so much against her own principles. And if it was true that her weakness had brought down the roof on herself, well, she was paying the price, she acknowledged unhappily, for the prospect of acting like Bastian's girlfriend around the barracuda was not an inviting one. Emmie would have been much happier had she never had to lay eyes on Bastian again but sadly that escape route wasn't open to her, and if she was uncomfortable now, it was also her fault for having allowed their relationship to become embarrassingly intimate, she reflected unhappily.

Bastian watched Emmie descend the stairs in a flowing blue maxi dress that matched her beautiful eyes. Five seconds later he was imagining a necklace of sapphires round her unadorned throat and five seconds after that he was meeting her eyes and registering that she might look like a goddess but she was a goddess of the iceberg variety, not the warm, chatty type. Frustration growled through Bastian, who was not in a good mood. So, he had got it wrong, so he had hurt her feelings, been less than tactful, but did she have to continue to hold that against him? He had apologised, hadn't he? As a male who rarely apologised he attached a great deal of significance to that apology. He watched Emmie's face light up with a sudden warm smile when the parents of the teenager who had knocked her flying into the pool the day before approached her and he noted the effort she was making to put his uncle and

aunt at ease. Lilah would still have been complaining
and nursing her bruises and making everyone around
her feel bad about the accident, but then Emmie, whatever else she was, didn't revel in being the centre of
attention. As Bastian sprang upright to go and greet
his supposed partner he saw Lilah's face tighten. No,
even Lilah hadn't counted on a beauty of Emmie's cali-
bre coming along to distract him, he conceded with a
shot of unexpected amusement. And that was all this
weird way he was feeling was, all the irrational thinking he had been doing and dwelling on mistakes, which
was *so* not his style, Bastian thought impatiently, gritting his teeth. Emmie was simply a distraction, a very
pleasant, very sexy distraction in the wake of the weeks
of media drama that Lilah had enjoyed whipping up.

Emmie saw Bastian first, breathtakingly handsome
in his pearl grey morning suit. Her heart skipped a
beat and her mouth ran dry and she really didn't want
to meet his eyes and was grateful when his uncle and
aunt engaged her in conversation. Over their shoulders, she glimpsed Bastian's ex, Lilah, staring at her
fixedly. Lilah was wearing a black and white frothy
bridesmaid dress that made her tiny figure look more
than ever like a delicate fairy's. Her heart-shaped face
and almond brown eyes glowed between the wings of
her waterfall-straight dark hair. She was quite exquisite in a dainty doll-like way and suddenly Emmie felt
like a great hulking giantess, standing as she did com-
fortably six feet tall in her heels.

'Emmie…' Bastian murmured, leaning close so that

his breath warmed her cheek and the scent of his cologne brought back a shattering memory of how it had
felt to be in his arms the night before when such a recollection was least welcome. He rested a light hand
against her spine, a contact that made her bristle like
a Rottweiler ready to attack. 'I'm relieved you're here.
I'm having a trying morning.'

'Misery loves company,' Emmie remarked, noting
the petulant expression Lilah was now sporting. Nessa
thought her brother's ex was a gold-digger but right
then, her own ego bruised as it was by Bastian's rough
treatment, Emmie thought he deserved to fall victim
to a gold-digger.

'Never a rose without a thorn,' Bastian quipped in
the same style, disconcerting Emmie with the come-
back.

'You actually have a sense of humour,' Emmie
noted, pleased by her tone of indifference, for he would
have had to torture her to get a warmer reaction out
of her.

'No, Lilah killed it. She arrived an hour ago and
upset Nessa within the first five minutes,' Bastian told
her wryly.

'Nessa will be fine. Your sister is worried about
you.' Although goodness knows why that would be,
said Emmie's inflection.

'All you have to do is act as though we're insepara-
ble,' Bastian informed her half under his breath.

'That's quite a challenge, Bastian.'

A hand closed over her slim shoulder as Bastian

turned her round, forcing her to collide with his glittering dark eyes. 'It wasn't a challenge for you last night, *glyka mou*.'

Last night? The discovery that he fought dirty did not surprise Emmie and mortified colour leapt into her cheeks, her brittle composure splintering at that full-on reminder of her weakness. 'Yes, but then I had drunk a little too much,' she countered in a forced whisper while smiling with determination at a couple walking past them. 'And even a frog could contrive to look like Prince Charming in the condition I was in.'

Bastian flipped her round to face him again. 'You were *not* drunk,' he ground out in an aggressive undertone.

'I don't see why it should bother you so much…you weren't the virgin who ended up with the frog!' Emmie snapped back at him vitriolically.

Smouldering black-lashed golden eyes assailed her, a line of dark colour suddenly accentuating his high cheekbones. His beautiful mouth compressed with iron control. 'I suggest we drop the subject.'

'You mentioned it first,' Emmie reminded him with spirit.

Bastian muttered something in Greek that sounded nasty.

'I'm sorry but I really do hate you,' Emmie confided shakily.

It was dawning on Bastian that the apology had not been worth its weight in gold or indeed in any currency, and he was genuinely quite shocked that he had not been able to charm Emmie into forgiving him. A fleet of limousines pulled up to take the bridal party and her relatives to the village church, and with difficulty Bastian suppressed his roaring sense of annoyance with the world in general to appreciate the pretty picture his kid sister made as she came down the stairs in her wedding dress.

Emmie sat silent in the limo driving them at a stately pace along the picturesque road, which was bounded by sandy beach on one side and olive groves and hills on the other. She wished she had not voiced that final outburst and longed even for better control over emotions that seemed to be operating on a terrifyingly high-powered level unfamiliar to her. But she had told Bastian the truth, the absolute truth: she *hated* him for even briefly thinking that she might be the kind of woman who sold her body for profit, but she hated herself for having succumbed to his dubious charms even more. Nor did she need a brain transplant to appreciate that Bastian Christou was not accustomed to being handed the frozen mitt—his expectation that his blue-blooded birth, power, influence and great wealth entitled him to more flattering treatment fairly shone from the tension in his bold bronzed profile.

The silence nibbled at her nerves and conscience reminded her that she had promised to deliver the companionship he had paid for. 'Where did Nessa meet Leonides?'

'She's known him all her life. His father is the island doctor. Nessa and Leonides started school together, went to uni in tandem and have been a couple virtually ever since.'

'That's so romantic,' Emmie commented. 'They must know each other so well.'

'But they're very young to be getting married,' Bastian remarked in a tone of disapproval. 'Nessa's already talking about starting a family.'

'Sometimes people know what they want at an early age. What age is she?'

'The same age as you. Have you similar dreams?' Bastian enquired a shade drily.

'Good grief, no!' Emmie declared with a grimace at the idea. 'I wouldn't know what to do with a husband or children. I'm a career girl.'

The pretty little church by the harbour was packed with well-wishers. Bastian settled Emmie into a front pew and left her there because he was standing as Leonides' best man. Emmie settled back to enjoy the unfamiliar Greek wedding ceremony, which seemed rather more colourful than the English version as the bearded priest swung his incense burner and chanted. Nessa looked ravishingly happy and, seeing the way bride and groom looked at each other, Emmie found that she was smiling until Lilah cast her a chilling glance over a bony shoulder that was pure malice. After posing for photos outside the church in the sunshine with Lilah moving closer to Bastian at every opportunity while giggling girlishly and clinging to his arm, Emmie could only think what bad taste in women Bastian had. Lilah was so horribly fake and gushy. Bastian might be extremely clever in business but he couldn't be the sharpest tool in the box when he had decided to marry a woman as artificial as Lilah.

The reception back at the house followed, caterers moving around with trays of champagne while Emmie stuck masochistically to water and simmered when Bastian raised a fine ebony brow as though mocking her abstinence. That man, she would surely have killed him outright for his audacity had he meant anything to her, which he *didn't*, she assured herself soothingly, taking a seat at the top table while Lilah watched Bastian fan out Emmie's napkin for her with sullen dark eyes.

'To forgive is divine,' Bastian teased.

'Men hate those they have hurt,' Emmie shot back at him thinly.

'But I don't hate you. You know, if you would try to be logical about this instead of emotional—'

'I am not *being* emotional,' Emmie seethed back at him, rage sparkling in her lovely eyes. He infuriated her. That she still thought he was gorgeous, found her gaze absently lingering on his spectacular bone structure or compelling eyes, only added fuel to her furious resentment.

'I think you're a *very* emotional individual,' Bastian returned with a derisive edge to his dark drawl.

'Better than having about as much feeling in me as a block of wood!'

Bastian watched his sister take to the floor with her new husband. Nessa was wreathed in smiles. The job

was done and his sister was content, he told himself
grimly. Why was he bothering to even try mending
fences with the most challenging woman he had ever
met? He had always avoided difficult, demanding personalities. His sister caught his eye and swivelled her
gaze towards Lilah, and Bastian stood up to lead the
chief bridesmaid onto the floor.

Emmie watched in consternation as Bastian led the
tiny brunette onto the dance floor. Lilah behaved like
a light that had been switched on full beam, all anima-
tion, smiles and chatter. Emmie's mouth folded down
at the corners. Maybe he *was* going to end up back
with his ex. They had been together a long time and
ties that close weren't easy to break. Maybe Emmie
had simply been a face-saving piece of arm candy on
Bastian's terms, retaliation because Lilah had broken
off their engagement. And Lilah *was* exquisite, there
was no denying that. Emmie watched the tiny brunette
nestle intimately into Bastian's tall powerful frame and
her hands knotted into fists below the table and her
teeth ground together. Typical guy, he had told her to
stick to him like glue to keep Lilah at bay and now he
was encouraging the other woman. Feeling hot moisture sting her eyes, Emmie was dismayed enough to
slide out of her chair and head for the powder room
off the main hall.

What on earth was the matter with her? She wasn't
jealous, had never been jealous of a man in her life.
No, all that was wrong with her was that she felt foolish and ashamed and humiliated that she had had sex

with Bastian. Satisfied with that explanation, Emmie returned to the hall and found Lilah squarely planted in her path.

'You're Emmie,' Lilah remarked with her cut-glass laugh.

And Emmie cringed, thinking, Good grief, he's told her he was with me last night! There was something so knowing and nasty about Lilah's scornful smile. 'And you're Lilah,' Emmie responded flatly.

'Bastian picked you up at the office, I believe—how sweet but how *lazy* of him. Men can be such bastards,' Lilah trilled like the evil fairy as Emmie stared down at the brunette feeling sick with embarrassment, guilt and discomfiture. 'He's using you to get at me. Don't you have any pride?'

'Don't you?' Emmie dared. 'We're not having this conversation.'

And Emmie swept on past, with her head held high, pale and trembling a little and grateful to have escaped Bastian's shrewish former fiancée. If the brunette had really cared for him would she ever have risked losing him in the first place? As Emmie crossed the room to Bastian's side she was seethingly conscious of his stunning dark golden gaze clinging to her. She mightn't like him but she *adored* his eyes. Suddenly it was hard to drag oxygen into her lungs and a flock of butterflies were dive-bombing her tummy. He reached out and closed a hand over hers to draw her close with an ease she resented. He seemed to feel no discomfiture at all over what had happened between them the night before.

Colour crawled up Emmie's cheeks, her nostrils flaring on the hot evocative scent of him that close to her, memory dragging her down and down so deep and fast she was lost within seconds. Her heartbeat quickened as she recalled the driving intensity of his body over and inside hers and an instant surge of heat snapped her nipples painfully tight and mushroomed in her pelvis.

'We need to talk, *glyka mou*,' Bastian breathed in a roughened undertone, but it was the very last thing he wanted to do. Her slender body was trembling infinitesimally beneath his arm and that close to the warmth of her he had an instant erection. Hunger was raging through him like a bush fire and all he wanted to do was drag her back to his bed and keep her there fully occupied until he felt normal again, cool again, *himself* again. Instead he thrust open the door into the conservatory and walked her in there.

'What are you doing?' Emmie demanded thinly. 'I don't want to be alone with you. The show of togetherness is only for public viewing!'

Smouldering golden eyes fringed by lush black lashes zeroed in on her. 'Stop fighting with me. It's childish. I apologised—'

'The man *apologised*!' Emmie scorned. 'I'm impressed.'

'You really do know how to press my buttons,' Bastian growled, golden eyes bright with anger as he hauled her into his arms. 'We start again afresh now—'

'No,' Emmie cut in, face uncertain and hectically pink as she looked up at him, fiercely resisting temptation. He had made a fool of her once; she wouldn't let him do it to her twice.

'I want you to be the same way you were with me last night,' Bastian admitted darkly.

'A tipsy stupid pushover?' Emmie snapped. 'Not a chance!'

He brought his hot devouring lips down on hers and it was like a lethal rocket attack on her treacherous body, sending a wave of melting heat to her feminine core with a kiss so boldly sexual and exciting that it left her head swimming and her knees weak. Her hands clutched at his shoulders to keep her upright, a drowning, quivering, overwhelming awareness engulfing her like a tide as her every skin cell lit up like a traffic light. He kept on kissing her, his tongue delving hungrily, one lean hand massaging the pouting curve of her breasts, releasing a whimper of sound from her throat as he rubbed her straining nipples through the fabric. His fingers reached down to yank up the skirt of her dress, trailed along her thigh and she froze, dragging her mouth free in desperation.

'No, Bastian.'

'Maybe some guys get off on rejection—I don't!' he bit out angrily.

The ache between her slender thighs hurt along with the knowledge that she could not satisfy her outrageous craving for him. 'Monday I'll be back at work for two short weeks and we pretend none of this ever happened…OK?' she pressed in desperation.

'If that's what you want,' Bastian framed between gritted teeth.

Emmie simply nodded. It *had* to be what she wanted. After all, no relationship between her and Bastian could go anywhere but the bedroom. He was a billionaire businessman, for goodness' sake, way out of her league and right now he was at a loose end and probably frustrated because he had a high-voltage libido and he was just out of a long relationship. All he could possibly want from her was sex and she refused to lower herself to that level. *A typical shag,* she reminded herself doggedly of his comment about his expectations of her the night before, which represented all too clearly how he saw her: as an escort for hire, an easy little office girl, surprising only in her lack of experience and currently the only available sexual option below his roof because most of his guests were his relatives.

He freed her and Emmie returned to the ballroom, shaken but determined to stay in control. She followed everyone else out to the big hall where Nessa stood on the upper landing of the stairs, posing for the hovering photographer to throw her bouquet. Twenty seconds later, the bouquet pitched down into Emmie's startled arms and Nessa whooped with satisfaction.

'I don't think so,' Lilah Siannas derided, treating Emmie to a contemptuous appraisal.

Emmie ignored the brunette and was literally watching the clock to calculate how soon she could excuse herself and retire to her room for the night. After all, once the bride and groom had departed, her role was surely at an end.

His simmering gaze pinned to Emmie's retreat up the stairs, Bastian knocked back a brandy without respecting the vintage and gritted his teeth: Emmie had thrown in the towel while Lilah was behaving like a demented stalker. Suddenly, Bastian was out of all patience with the entire female sex and he crossed the room to join his grandfather and make a suggestion about how they could best spend what remained of the night. Theron's lean weathered face lit up in surprise and pleasure.

'No, I don't want to talk about it,' he told the old man grimly.

Emmie wakened when a maid brought her breakfast. She had slept like a log, exhausted by the strain of keeping up a front on Nessa's wedding day. In the warmth of the sunlight now filling the room, she felt stronger and brighter, and she took a quick shower to freshen up before sitting down at the table out on the balcony where her breakfast awaited her. The view of the empty beach and the turquoise sea arched over by a clear blue sky was fantastic. A text beeped on her cell phone and she lifted it.

'Be ready to leave at nine. I will not be travelling with you. Thank you for your assistance.'

It was from Bastian, no *x* at the end, nothing personal. A sharp sense of disappointment pierced Emmie and she questioned her response. After all, her role was at an end and as she had refused Bastian the night before he naturally saw no point in further contact with her. She was once again the woman he had hired to do a job and the job was done, she reminded herself painfully, disconcerted that her eyes were filling with stinging tears. What the heck was wrong with her? This was how the cookie crumbled when he was a billionaire and she was an office worker…unless she fell pregnant, a little voice whispered in the back of her mind, sending a cooling shiver of consternation through her. With that possibility in mind it might be more sensible to be a little less aggressive in her attitude to him, she reasoned unhappily, and she stood up, wondering if Bastian was still in his room. Not even sure of what she planned to say, she went to the door between their rooms on impulse and knocked. She was shocked when the door jerked open to reveal Lilah.

'Oh…' Emmie breathed, losing colour and falling back a step.

A complacent smile on her lips, Lilah preened in the doorway, making the most of Emmie's surprise at her being in Bastian's bedroom.

'You're being sent straight back to London,' Lilah pointed out as though her presence in Bastian's room and Emmie's travel itinerary were connected, which very probably they were, Emmie reflected with a sinking heart and a despondent sense of humiliation. If Bastian was back with his ex, Emmie was too much of an embarrassing extra to keep below the same roof.

'Yes,' Emmie agreed with no expression at all, too

proud to betray her mortification to the other woman but feeling vindicated in her decision not to take Bastian's apparent interest in her seriously the night before. Evidently he was back in the arms of his ex. That hadn't taken long. Bastian had been on the rebound; that was the only reason he had come after her but, clearly and understandably, it was Lilah whom he had *really* wanted. For no reason that she could comprehend, Emmie felt gutted, absolutely gutted by that obvious fact.

The door closed. Dry-eyed, facial muscles locked tight, Emmie packed her case. She had better hope she wasn't pregnant for, in this situation, what a disaster such an unwelcome development would be!

CHAPTER SEVEN

THREE WEEKS LATER, Emmie ripped open a pregnancy-testing kit during her break at the café and pulled out the instruction leaflet. Her heart was beating as fast as a drum, sheer tension slicking her taut face with a sheen of perspiration. After all, she was already homeless and pretty much jobless and she most definitely did not need to be pregnant into the bargain. Admittedly, she had sore breasts and was feeling sick round the clock. But so what? It was a bug she had picked up some place, a stupid bug, she told herself frantically.

At the same time, in the considerably greater comfort of his office in the City, Bastian was tossing aside his phone after contacting Emmie's mother, Odette Taylor. That had proved to be a fruitless call. Evidently Emmie had moved out without leaving a forwarding address and her fond parent neither knew nor cared where she had gone. That was the point when Bastian realised that he had hit a brick wall. Of course, he hadn't expected to learn that Emmie had already left his employ when he arrived back in London but he still *had* to see her, had to check she was all right. He owed her that consideration at least, Bastian reasoned grimly, and as far as he was aware his PA, Marie, was the only member of his staff who had got to know Emmie in any depth. He called the efficient brunette in and after a couple of going-nowhere minutes of tactful probing lost patience and simply admitted that he wanted to contact Emmie.

Back in the tiny café staffroom, Emmie scanned the test wand again with swimming eyes. She wanted to sob and scream like a little child for the pregnancy test had proved positive and for a couple of shameful minutes nothing less than terror controlled Emmie. A *baby*…she was going to have a *baby* and the pregnancy was already making her as sick as a dog! She felt awful, truly awful! And yet she couldn't contemplate a termination because she was all too well aware that had Odette had that option, neither she nor her sisters might ever have been born. Didn't her baby deserve love and appreciation? She could not reject her child simply because the timing didn't suit, the pregnancy was unplanned and she had no supportive man in the picture. Emmie released her breath on a dismissive hiss on that latter score. With the single exception of Kat, neither Emmie nor her siblings had enjoyed the advantage of a caring father in their lives.

'It's getting busy out here!' her boss called through the door to bring her break to an early conclusion.

Emmie straightened her overall, locked her bag away again and returned to work. She had no choice now but to go home to her sister, Kat, she reflected guiltily. At present she was sleeping on a friend's sofa and she wasn't earning enough at the café to pay rent and eat at the same time. Kat ran a guesthouse in the Lake District and would probably be glad to have help with the cleaning and catering, Emmie thought, striving for a more positive angle than a daunting image of herself being forced to run home like a helpless teenager, who couldn't cope with the adult world. Of course she could have approached her sister Saffy for assistance: Saffy owned an apartment in London. But the prospect of asking for help from her very much more successful twin was too humiliating for Emmie. She could not imagine the shrewd and worldly-wise Saffy ever making such a basic mistake as to fall accidentally pregnant. In short Emmie literally cringed at the idea of having to admit to her twin how very badly her own move to London had gone for her.

Bastian was able to pick Emmie out from across the café. She wore a candy-pink overall that was a little too short for such a leggy young woman and she looked incredibly pale. Maybe she just wasn't wearing make-up, he reasoned, taking a seat in a booth while still studying her tall slender figure. Her head turned, treating him to a flash of dazzling blue eyes, luscious pink lips parting to show a glimpse of the oddly enticing gap between her two front teeth. His body, recently proven to be woodenly impervious to the charms of more available women, reacted with an instant arousal that set his teeth on edge. Emmie saw him and stilled in obvious dismay. Bastian smiled regardless, shifted lean brown fingers in fluid invitation, mentally willing her to move in his direction.

The potent pull of Bastian in the flesh was so powerful that Emmie felt as if she were being yanked across the floor by a force stronger than she was. She approached him reluctantly, notepad in hand, mouth dry, every muscle strained taut. 'What are you doing here?' she asked breathlessly.

'When do you finish?'

Emmie collided with dark golden eyes as compelling as chains snaking out to entrap her body. She supposed there was no avoiding what had to be faced. He had a right to know about the pregnancy. His preference for Lilah did not enter the equation because that was personal, *his* personal business. All that should really matter to Emmie was that she was carrying his child; however the shock of that discovery was still rippling through her like the aftermath of an earthquake. 'My shift ends at ten.'

'I'll be waiting.' Without further ado, Bastian sprang up and strode outside: decisive, impatient, stubbornly practical, she affixed ruefully. She knew he would have demanded she leave right now in the middle of her shift had he believed he could bully her into doing so.

When she emerged from the café at closing time a limousine was parked by the kerb.

'Miss Marshall?' the driver asked out of the window before getting out to whip open the passenger door for her. Emmie swallowed hard, struggled to suppress the nausea in her stomach, and climbed in. She was disconcerted by the discovery that the limo was empty and asked Bastian's driver where he was taking her.

'I'm to drive you back to Mr Christou's apartment.'

Emmie pushed her weary head back against the headrest. She didn't care at the moment where she was going, was only grateful that she did not have to walk there. If she had to make her big announcement, it was better to do so where they would not be overheard or interrupted. How would he react? Would he be angry, resentful, bitter? Would he offer to pay for a termination or even suggest adoption as an alternative? The driver escorted her into a luxury block of apartments and, tucking her into a lift, pressed the correct button for her.

Bastian impatiently paced the wooden floor of his elegant lounge. He was convinced that he knew what she was going to tell him: he had suspected the truth the minute her strained eyes had met his. Three weeks ago, Emmie had been considerably more cheerful and calm and he could not credit that escaping her harpy of a mother had left her in such low spirits. Now Bastian, who was confident that he excelled at solving problems, was bent on working out how he could best turn an apparent negative into a positive.

A man in a suit had the door of Bastian's apartment standing open for her arrival when she stepped out of the lift into a stylishly decorated hallway. Crossing it, Emmie tightened the sash on her raincoat and dug her nervous hands into her pockets, pushing her shoulders back as she entered the dimly lit apartment, noting the long expanses of window that denoted a penthouse, the clean lines of sleek contemporary furniture and the same lack of clutter that distinguished Bastian's office. Even on that level they didn't suit each other, Emmie mused, for she was a great hoarder of sentimental bits and pieces.

Bastian strode forward. 'Take your coat off. Make yourself comfortable,' he urged huskily.

Emmie flicked a glance at his lean, darkly handsome face and the lustrous brilliance of his dark, thickly lashed eyes and turned pink and uncomfortable. He was spectacularly good-looking and had the most colossal impact on her every time she saw him. Heat flickering like an uneasy flame low in her pelvis, she undid her coat, shrugged it off, sat down, and pressed her knees and her hands together like a child urged to be on her very best behaviour. 'It's not good news,' she told him awkwardly.

Bastian's gaze roamed across her flawless face and down over the elegant lines of her willowy figure with instinctive appreciation. There was something special about her and he still didn't know what it was but it was a quality that shouted at him every time he saw her. 'That depends on how you look at it.'

'I'm pregnant,' Emmie delivered curtly. 'And no matter how you look at it, it's a problem. I don't want a child right now when I'm only at the start of my career and yet I couldn't live with having an abortion just because it's a case of bad timing—'

'*I* could take the baby,' Bastian interrupted.

Thoroughly taken aback by that suggestion, Emmie lifted her head and stared back at him with bright blue eyes of disbelief. 'You can't be serious?'

'Why not? I was prepared to get married to have a family. How is this situation different?'

'If you had married, you would have had a wife—'

'Don't be prejudiced. I would make an excellent single father. Certainly, I know all the things a father *shouldn't* do,' Bastian proffered with brutal honesty. 'My father was an appalling role model.'

'So was mine...er—'

'All I'm saying is that if you don't want the baby, I *do*—'

'I didn't say I didn't want it!' Emmie protested, dismayed by his attitude and suddenly feeling ridiculously protective of the new life forming inside her. And yet on another level, she respected him for his unexpected willingness to get involved and take responsibility. 'I think it's just that I don't know what to do *now*.'

'We don't have to make any serious decisions for months yet,' Bastian pointed out soothingly.

'I *do* want my baby,' Emmie started to confide but her tummy was rolling about like a ship on a stormy sea and she was forced to leap back upright. 'Where's the cloakroom?' she gasped in dismay.

Luckily, she made it there in time and was sick for the second time that evening. Afterwards, limp and drained, she leant across the vanity unit to freshen up and peered at her bloodshot eyes and extreme pallor in the mirror. She looked like death warmed over, she conceded painfully.

'Should I call a doctor?' Bastian greeted her right outside the door, which embarrassed her. 'Take you to a hospital?'

'No, I assume this is what the books call morning sickness, only it seems to strike me at all hours of the day,' Emmie told him morosely, rubbing her cheeks on the recollection of how pale she had looked and then wondering why she was bothering…as if *that* were going to make a difference and transform her from a humble waitress clad in an ugly overall into a sexually appealing woman! Why on earth would she even want to appeal to him now?

'I didn't think you would be affected by anything of that nature this early,' Bastian remarked.

'That makes two of us, but I already feel pretty sick most of the time.'

'Where are you staying at the minute?' Bastian asked.

Emmie reddened and sat down again. 'How did you know I'd moved out of my mother's flat?'

'I tried to contact you there.'

'She was still trying to get me to accept bookings from her clients,' Emmie admitted reluctantly. 'I had no choice but to leave.'

'I thought she would continue to put you under pressure. Where are you currently staying?' he asked again.

Emmie admitted she was sleeping on a sofa at a friend's house. 'There's not much else I can do. I'm not earning enough to pay rent,' she admitted stiffly, mortified by the difference in their financial situations but determined to be as honest as she could be.

Bastian's face tensed, his wildly sensual mouth compressing into a taut line. 'That *is* something I can help with. I own several apartments for the use of employees flying in from abroad. You can move into one of them.'

Emmie frowned. 'I couldn't possibly—'

'Of course you can,' Bastian cut in firmly. 'I'm responsible for the situation you're in. It's the least I can do.'

Emmie swallowed hard on the pride threatening to choke her. The prospect of sleeping on a sofa for another night had little appeal and she couldn't possibly inconvenience her friend by staying with her for much longer. Being homeless was frightening, Emmie acknowledged wretchedly. The security of a roof over her head would give her a much-needed breathing space, which she could use to decide what to do next. 'OK, but I'm only agreeing because I don't have any other option.'

Bastian pulled his phone out and spoke to someone at length in his own language. 'The place will be fully stocked for your use by the time we arrive,' he asserted. 'Give me the address where you have been staying and I will arrange to have your belongings conveyed to the apartment for you.'

He made everything sound so easy. Although she could not help being impressed she also knew that nothing could have better illustrated the vast gulf between them—the extent of his wealth and power versus her poverty and lack of influence. Only that did not mean she had to be weak or meek, she reflected, tilting her chin. But sometimes accepting a helping hand when life was tough was the most sensible move.

Two hours later, Bastian gave Emmie a tour of the apartment he had offered her. It contained every luxury she could think of, from a stock of DVDs and a power shower to a fridge freezer stocked with every necessity. 'I'll be very comfortable here,' Emmie remarked carefully. 'But you have to promise to tell me when you need it for someone who works for you.'

Dark golden eyes accentuated by luxuriant black lashes focused on her intently and her heart hammered hard beneath her breastbone. 'Right now, your needs are more important. Let's face it, that's *my* baby you're carrying,' he traded levelly. 'Naturally you're my first priority.'

The possessive note of that comment about the baby disconcerted her. Her soft pink lips parted. 'Is that really how you feel? Do you like children?'

'Never really thought about it. I don't *dislike* them,' Bastian declared pensively. 'But the child you have, whether it's a boy or a girl, will be my heir.'

'Even though we're not married?'

'It will still be my child with my blood in its veins.'

There was something rather basic and territorial about that statement and Emmie was even more surprised. She recognised that he had not only adapted to the idea of becoming a father but had also warmed to the prospect.

'To be blunt, I've never been in a hurry to get married,' Bastian admitted drily. 'Watching my father screw up matrimonially four times over soured me on the institution.'

'I can understand that. So you think that having a child without having to tie yourself down to marriage might actually suit you better?' Emmie queried, keen to understand his point of view.

'Only time will answer that question. In the morning I'll make enquiries and organise an obstetrician for you,' Bastian continued. 'You must have proper medical care.'

'You can be very…bossy.' Emmie selected the label with care, because in spite of the shock news she had given him he had been remarkably kind and considerate and she didn't want to seem ungrateful.

A wicked grin that was the very essence of masculine charisma sliced across Bastian's beautifully shaped and stubborn mouth. 'You could say that being dominant comes naturally to me, *glyka mou*. Or even beware of Greeks bearing gifts,' he teased.

'Needs must when the devil rides,' she quoted, her gaze compulsively welded to that grin, and she was as short of breath as if all the oxygen had been sucked out of the atmosphere.

'I'm not the devil. I only want to do what's best for you,' Bastian told her thickly, staring down at her with smouldering golden eyes.

Emmie felt her treacherous body react to his proximity and the husky, sexy note in his deep voice. Her nipples tingled, awareness washing through her in an exhilarating overload of sudden sexual energy. But this time, Emmie fought what she was feeling to the last ditch. She stepped hurriedly back from him, her cheeks burning as she deliberately turned her head away from him to avoid eye contact. She was hugely attracted to him but could not forget his renewed intimacy with Lilah on the night of his sister's wedding. Although there had been no reference in the gossip columns to a reconciliation between Bastian and his former fiancée, Emmie didn't want to risk getting more deeply involved with a man already entangled with another woman. Wasn't it worrying enough that she was pregnant by him? The last thing she needed now was to let her overwrought emotions persuade her that she was in some way attached to Bastian Christou.

'Emmie…' he breathed thickly, stroking a fingertip very lightly over the back of her hand, making her quiver and long to twist round and hurl herself into his arms like a lovesick fool. But she *wasn't* lovesick and she *wasn't* a fool, she told herself fiercely.

'Let's not complicate things,' Emmie pleaded in a charged undertone. She found him almost impossible to resist but there was such a thing as common sense and it was way past time she exerted it over her more self-destructive promptings. And going to bed with Bastian again would definitely come under the heading of destructive, she thought painfully.

Bastian closed a strong hand to her shoulder and turned her back to face him. Diamond-bright dark eyes locked to hers enquiringly. 'We're already complicated.'

'Exactly, and you're helping me out here, which I'm very grateful for,' she said shakily. 'But—'

His winged black brows drew together. 'Just as you didn't expect diamonds, I'm not expecting any kind of reward for helping out,' he told her drily.

Discomfited at the way he had interpreted her statement, Emmie reddened. 'That wasn't what I meant.'

Bastian had her cornered in the hall, his lean, powerful body squarely planted between her and the front door. 'Then what did you mean?' he pressed.

Emmie jerked an awkward shoulder in the tense silence that had fallen. 'I know you slept with Lilah the night of the wedding—'

Bastian lifted a frowning black brow, dark eyes widening in surprise. 'No, I didn't—'

'She was in your room the next morning.'

'But I *wasn't*,' Bastian riposted with hard emphasis. 'I spent the night at my grandfather's and we sat up playing poker until the early hours. I lost a packet to the wily old buzzard too. If Lilah was in my room she was there uninvited. Think about it, Emmie. Do you think I'm such a fool that I would hire you to keep her at bay and then get back into bed with her again?'

Emmie didn't know what to think. 'She even knew that I was leaving the island—'

'Anyone in the house could have given her that information as I made the arrangements for your departure with my staff before I left the night before.' Bastian frowned down at her and slowly shook his handsome head. 'Obviously Lilah would have wanted you to think that I had been with her and she knew that I was spending the night at Theron's. I can't believe you fell for it.'

Mortified by that assessment, Emmie said nothing. The doorbell buzzed and Bastian yanked the door open. The suitcase she had taken to her friend's house was carted over the threshold. 'Is this all that you have?' Bastian asked in surprise.

'No, I left some stuff boxed up at my mother's,' Emmie admitted wryly.

'I'll sort that out for you as well,' Bastian declared, carrying the case into the bedroom and then striding back to the front door with an air of relief. 'I'll phone you tomorrow…check that you're all right.'

And that fast he was gone and Emmie was left blinking at the space he had occupied and guiltily suppressing a strong sense of disappointment. Her bringing up the subject of Lilah and falsely accusing him had evidently stifled any desire on his part to make their relationship more intimate, she registered ruefully. Had he truly spent that night at his grandfather's house?

'There are two heartbeats,' the obstetrician informed Emmie. 'You're carrying twins.'

'Twins?' Emmie listened transfixed to the galloping pace of her babies' heartbeats. She was only eight weeks into her pregnancy and was amazed at how much could already be seen on a scan.

'I think this is why you've been feeling so sick. Severe nausea is more common with a twin pregnancy,' the older man informed her.

Emmie rested her head back down and wondered how Bastian would react to the news. The prospect of two babies unnerved her, raised as she had been on horror stories of how hard her mother had found it to cope with twins. Her heart sank as a rather more practical concern struck her: how many years would it be before she could hope to earn enough to afford childcare for *two* children? And if she couldn't earn enough, how would she ever get her independence back? Was she destined to live off Bastian's largesse for years to come?

For the present, Bastian was keeping her and Emmie wasn't comfortable with that arrangement, no matter how often he pointed out that the baby that was putting her out of commission with nausea was as much his responsibility as hers. During the past two weeks while Emmie struggled to cope with the almost constant sickness, which even medication had failed to banish, Bastian had become a surprisingly regular visitor. He would call in to check up on her on his way home, sometimes he would order in food for them both and stay a while and on two occasions he had sent the limo to pick her up and bring her back to his penthouse to enjoy a meal cooked by his housekeeper. The new relationship they had forged had limits though, Emmie acknowledged tautly. Bastian would ask her how her visit to the obstetrician he had engaged had gone but he wouldn't accompany her or make his questions too personal. In the same way he had made no further attempt to renew the intimacy they had so briefly enjoyed.

Spending time with Bastian on a platonic basis, however, was torture for Emmie and she was thoroughly ashamed of that truth. It was as though, having been programmed to react to him once, her body could not learn how to block the signals of attraction. She had to consciously will herself not to stare at him, not to lean closer, indeed not to touch him in any way. It disconcerted her that even feeling unwell couldn't stifle the strong sexual feelings Bastian still awakened in her.

Before she could lose her nerve she texted her news to Bastian, reasoning that that was less emotional than telling him face to face.

'Had scan. We're having twins,' ran her text.

And the text was sent before she could think better of using that royal 'we' as if they were a couple, rather than two very different people attempting to find common ground as potential parents on the strength of an accidental pregnancy.

Twins? An unholy grin of satisfaction illuminated Bastian's lean dark features in the midst of the meeting he was chairing. He totally forgot what he had been saying while texting back a one-word response. Emmie was having two babies and he thought that was terrific news. He had been a lonely only child for more years than he cared to count but *his* child would have company and a sibling to play with. He left the meeting to instruct Marie to send Emmie flowers. He saw the flash of surprise in his PA's face when she heard the name and realised where Emmie was living and frowned, wishing he could bring the relationship out of the closet. Unfortunately, Emmie didn't want people gossiping about them and preferred to stay in the background of his life while totally ignoring the reality that a child could not be hidden indefinitely.

Bastian, however, didn't want to stage an argument with Emmie and lay down the law. How could he when she was getting so thin he would do almost anything to persuade her to eat a decent meal? Her doctor had given her medication but it had yet to provide a cure. Before his very eyes the constant sickness was wearing her health down, stripping away her delicate curves, giving her face a pinched look. Concealing his concern, respecting the boundaries set by someone else went against the grain with Bastian, but he continually told himself that it would all be worth it for the end result.

After all, all his life he had dreaded the idea of getting married, fearing that he would somehow repeat his father's mistakes. He had deemed Lilah a safe choice, only realising what a nightmare she could be *after* they had parted. Conversely, Bastian choosing to stay single and childless would devastate his grandfather, who was obsessed with the continuation of the family tree. But, quite unexpectedly, Emmie was giving Bastian the best of both worlds: a child without the risk and the restrictions of marriage. Theron would be shocked that Bastian's children were illegitimate but Bastian was convinced that however he felt the old man would not ignore his great-grandchildren's arrival into the world.

'Fantastic…' ran Bastian's text and it came back too fast in response to Emmie's announcement to be a polite fiction.

CHAPTER EIGHT

EMMIE SMILED WITH pleasure at Bastian's very positive reaction and on impulse texted him back again inviting him to join her for dinner. She wasn't a versatile cook but she could manage a decent steak. She was even more pleased when Bastian's flowers arrived. Having set the table in the alcove off the lounge, she changed into the dress she had worn the night before Nessa's wedding. Although it was a much tighter fit over her enlarged breasts, the rest of her was as slender as ever and the zip went up easily.

Bastian was punctual and she hurried to answer the door. His brilliant dark-lashed eyes roamed over her leggy figure in the fuchsia-pink dress and she blushed furiously, embarrassed that she had gone to so much trouble to make the most of her appearance.

'Are we celebrating?' Bastian enquired, studying her with hungry intensity. 'I love that dress.'

'You seemed pleased about the twins,' Emmie pointed out awkwardly, feeling painfully self-conscious with his full attention trained to her. Her nipples prickled and lengthened, the sensitive tips scraping against the lace cup of the bra cupping the full mounds. A clenching sensation low in her pelvis made her press her thighs together and squirm with shame. Without even trying Bastian lit her up like a bonfire inside, she acknowledged in fierce mortification.

Something primal flamed and smouldered in the depth of Bastian's dark deep-set eyes and without warning he reached for her, pulling her into the hard, unyielding heat of his lean, powerful body. His mouth plunged down in hot, urgent demand on hers. Excitement exploded through Emmie and she couldn't breathe for the wild clamour of her thundering heart and the heightened effect on her senses.

'Tell me yes…' Bastian growled into her hair as she snatched in a quivering breath, struggling not to shudder in reaction as he ran lean fingers up a slender thigh below the hem of her dress, roving tantalisingly close to the source of the intimate ache making her so tense. '*Yes*, you want this as much as I do.'

The solid ridge of his arousal was potent and compelling against her stomach, and that he could hunger for her that much made desire leap inside her while moisture gathered in readiness at the heart of her. Weak as a newborn as that wild surge of yearning engulfed her, her fingers biting into his shoulders, she leant into him. 'Yes…' she whispered, no longer able to suppress her natural inclinations, frantic to feel him moving inside her again, awakening her to a level of sensation she had never known possible. 'Yes…'

And Bastian required no further invitation. He lifted her up into his arms and carried her through to the bedroom, sinking down on the mattress with her across his lap as he unzipped her dress. 'I feel like I've waited for ever for you, *glyka mou.*'

Emmie lifted her fingers to rest them gently against his stubborn, wilful and utterly beautiful mouth, trembling as he parted his lips and sucked on her fingertips. 'You're not used to waiting, I'm not used to giving.'

And it was true, for she had too often played safe simply to protect herself from the risk of hurt and rejection, but something about Bastian destroyed her defences, blew her heart wide open, made her want to *give* instead. She met eyes ablaze with sexual hunger and marvelled that she had the power to make him feel that way. Another kiss and he was stripping off her dress, peeling away her bra to curve gentle caressing fingers to her swollen nipples, his every touch sending fire to her aching core.

Emmie twisted against Bastian, fingers clenching into his luxuriant hair to hold him close while she kissed him with all the passion she had repressed for so long. Quick to get the message that speed could be an advantage, Bastian kissed her fervently back while also hauling off his jacket, ditching his tie and embarking on his shirt buttons. She spread reverent fingers across his hard-muscled bronzed torso, appreciating the lithe strength and raw masculinity of his powerful body. He lifted her off him, disposed of his well-cut pants and stretched out beside her on the bed, but he lay still for barely a second before he sat up again to study her semi-naked length with burnished eyes of appreciation.

'I want you so much it's painful to hold back,' Bastian groaned, a fingertip toying teasingly with the shallow indentation of her belly button, and then straying down over her mound to more responsive territory and skating over the taut, damp triangle of material stretched beneath.

Emmie's back arched and her hips writhed as he touched her, fierce hunger pounding through her like a pagan drum beat that filled her ears and her thoughts so that she was aware of nothing beyond the wicked skill of his hands on her unbearably tender flesh. He whisked away the last barrier and, parting the delicate pink folds, he thrust a finger into her aching core. She gasped, twisted and turned, wanted him so much it physically pained her to withstand such teasing.

'I want to watch you come this time,' Bastian confided thickly, sliding down the bed to caress the engorged buds of her nipples with his mouth and his tongue while at the same time he drove her crazy with every plunge of his fingers.

Emmie couldn't stay still. She was on fire for him, quivering with excitement and a level of need that came close to torment. 'Bastian, *please*,' she whimpered.

And he lifted her up and sank into her so hard and deep and fast that she cried out with excitement.

Bastian groaned with sensual satisfaction. 'Hot… wet…tight, *khriso mou*, my every dream come true.'

Emmie was on a high of rapturous sensation. He rode her with abandon, pleasuring her with hard rapid strokes that stoked her excitement to feverish heights. She was out of control, her heart thundering as she flew high on his erotic rhythm, her body rising to meet his. At the apex of her climax she convulsed around him, shattering in the devouring waves of pleasure that consumed her.

'On a scale of one to ten that was an eleven, *khriso mou*,' Bastian breathed raggedly, releasing her from his weight only to snake an arm round her and hold her captive to his long lean length.

His comment jarred, slicing like a blade through the cosy cocoon of relaxation Emmie's body was embracing, because she was too well aware that in bed she had nobody she could compare him to. It made her feel cheap to think he might be comparing her to past lovers and she stiffened defensively.

Her movement made Bastian look down at the arms he still had wrapped round her restless body. Faint colour accentuating his high cheekbones because he was uncomfortable with his own unfamiliar behaviour, he freed her abruptly, but not before he had dropped a kiss on her furrowed brow.

'So where do we go from here?' Emmie prompted.

Bastian hated questions like that and he thought it was typical that Emmie would put him on the spot and want immediate answers. 'It's just sex,' he parried very drily. 'Let's not get too worked up about it.'

Face burning in receipt of that demeaning response, Emmie froze and gritted her teeth together.

Bastian knew he had said the wrong thing but he was too arrogant to take it back. He also didn't know the answer to her question and was already mentally sidestepping all the many complications he imagined lay ahead of them. She was carrying his kids and that made her much more than a lover. He tensed, not in the mood to think about that reality and suddenly very keen to be distracted from such troublesome and confusing thoughts.

'Let's go out to eat,' he suggested abruptly.

'I was going to make a meal.'

Bastian didn't want to share an intimate meal in the apartment because he foresaw more difficult questions hovering like storm clouds on his horizon. 'I can't stay long,' he told her, sliding out of the bed with fluid grace. 'I'm flying to Australia tomorrow and moving on into Asia to check our operations there. I'll be away for a while.'

Taken aback by this first reference to his imminent departure, Emmie sat up, feeling ridiculously lonely and lost. *It's just sex.* His bronzed profile was hard and taut, his tension palpable to her. He didn't want her attaching fancy labels to their lovemaking or attaching strings of commitment to him. She might be pregnant with his babies and he might still want to have rampant sex with her, but he was not prepared to offer her a more serious relationship. Had she really expected anything else? All over again she had tumbled into bed with Bastian without thinking about what she was doing, without worrying about how he thought of her or wondering about where it would lead.

Bastian's silence, his patent eagerness to leave gave her an answer she really didn't want. A hard lump filled her throat and she couldn't swallow. She felt hurt, desperately hurt and rejected. Obviously she wanted more from Bastian than she was currently receiving. Equally obviously she had been in proud denial of what he could make her feel. Yet again she had ignored the clear limits of their association, for she dared not call it a relationship.

'If you don't feel like going out, I'll order food in,' Bastian volunteered, buttoning his shirt, grabbing up his jacket.

In that moment she hated him more than any man alive. 'I've already eaten,' she lied.

'You know you need to be eating more when you're being so sick,' Bastian reminded her darkly.

Sensing his impatience, Emmie simply nodded agreement. 'You order,' she advised, snaking out of bed to snatch up her dressing gown and vanish into the bathroom.

She had never felt less hungry in her life, she acknowledged wretchedly. *It's just sex.* Those three words had ripped her apart and forced her to re-examine the consequences of allowing Bastian to pay her bills and maintain a roof over her head. Did he see her as something less now? Had he ever had any respect for her? *It's just sex.* Even worse, did he now think of her as his mistress? How did a very rich man regard a woman whom he was already keeping? Certainly not as an equal. Emmie knew she had a big nasty decision to make but she would have to handle that later when Bastian had gone. Right then the bravest thing she had ever done in her life was shelve all her messy emotions, walk back out of the bathroom, throw on the only jeans that still fitted her and join him in the lounge where he was already ensconced watching the business news.

Korean food was delivered. While he watched she nibbled, chased the food round her plate, drank a lot of water. 'You need to eat more,' Bastian told her again and he leant out of his chair to close a big hand round her thin forearm. 'You're getting ridiculously skinny.'

Hot colour splashed her cheeks and then receded again as she wondered if he found that thinness unattractive. Her bright blue eyes rested on his handsome features, lingering on the spiky black lashes shading his dark golden gaze, the strong blade of his nose, the hard cheekbones and the beautifully modelled mouth. She swallowed hard, taking a mental snapshot of him because she already knew it would be a long time, if ever, before she saw him again.

'I'll phone when I can,' Bastian told her at the front door, looking down at her, wondering how she could look so beautiful and yet so painfully vulnerable at the same time, wishing he could take her abroad with him to give him something to look forward to at night other than an empty hotel suite. She needed looking after though, not foreign travel, he acknowledged grudgingly, and he had never looked after anyone before and didn't quite know where or how to begin.

Tears trickled down Emmie's face as she checked the train times online to plan her journey home to the Lake District. It would be madness to stay where she was when she and Bastian wanted such different things. She wanted more than sex from Bastian but she suspected that he still saw her as little more than the escort he had hired at such great expense to attend his sister's wedding with him. How on earth had she contrived to fall in love with him? He might be great in bed but he had to be the most insensitive man alive! And yet Bastian's constant phone calls and visits had still become ridiculously precious to Emmie in recent weeks. She blinked back the tears, ashamed of her weakness, her wanton desire to stay on in London and settle for whatever he was offering. Bastian was being as supportive as he knew how because it was his fault she was pregnant. Beyond that did he feel anything for her but basic sexual attraction? And how long would that last once she began to resemble a blimp? No, Emmie told herself angrily, she had to cut the connection and leave while she still had her pride. Sleeping with Bastian again had been a serious mistake but staying on in an apartment he owned would be an even worse mistake.

'Emmie's moved out…are you sure?' Bastian growled down the phone at his PA. After months of unanswered calls and considerable concern on his part he had finally caved in and asked Marie to check Emmie's apartment for him.

'Well, the wardrobe and the drawers are empty but she's left her teddy collection behind in a box on the bed,' Marie told him, working tactfully at keeping the amusement out of her voice. 'Oh, wait a minute, there's an envelope here with your name on it. Looks like she's left you a note.'

Bastian wanted to know very badly what was in the note but he refused to ask his PA to open it and read it to him over the phone. Some things were private. On the other side of the world he stared blankly at the wall of his hotel suite: *Emmie had walked out on him*. Rage momentarily electrified him. *Diavelos*, she was expecting his kids, she had no right to stage a disappearance when he had been doing everything possible to make her feel happy and secure! Well, possibly not *everything*, conscience bade him admit, discomfiture infiltrating his angry sense of betrayal.

In the following months since Emmie had travelled to visit her sister Kat, everything had turned out very differently from what Emmie had initially expected, she reflected wryly, while conceding that different didn't necessarily mean bad.

Firstly, her plan to help her sister run her guesthouse had died the very first day when Kat admitted that business was very poor and she was actually on the brink of bankruptcy. Luckily, a very wealthy Russian had come out of the woodwork to save the day for her sister. Mikhail Kusnirovich had invited Kat to stay on his mega yacht and act as hostess to his guests. While Kat was away Emmie stayed on in the farmhouse to keep her youngest sister, Topsy, company during the school holidays. A few weeks later, Kat admitted that she and Mikhail had fallen in love and that she was moving into his Georgian country mansion, Danegold Hall, to live with him as his partner. Within months Mikhail and Kat were married.

Denied her elder sister's company aside of occasional weekends spent in the lap of luxury at Danegold, Emmie had been thrown very much on her own resources. She had taken a temporary job as a shop assistant in a local supermarket but was currently engaged in looking into the possibility of opening a gift shop/café in a property available for rent in the village. Her new brother-in-law, Mikhail, had blithely offered her unlimited funds with which to start up her own business.

'I don't care what it costs me. Kat's worried sick about you. If she sees that you're making a new start in life on a decent income, she'll stop worrying about you being a single parent,' Mikhail had told Emmie cheerfully, not even trying to hide the reality that his main motivation was to make her sister happy.

As the months passed and her pregnancy advanced, Emmie had suffered less from nausea, and holding down a job and working regular hours had become a good deal easier. Yet when her twin, Saffy, had announced that she was remarrying her first husband,

Zahir, Emmie had used her health as an excuse not to attend the wedding and she was still ashamed of that. Her sister was now the wife of the King of Maraban and a future queen. And as Saffy had always enjoyed a good deal of natural dignity and assurance, Emmie believed her sibling would be a stunning success as a royal. Unfortunately, Emmie's own deep unhappiness had persuaded her that she would be a sad spectre at the feast if she attended her twin's wedding and that she would only cast an unwelcome pall of gloom over her sister's big day. When all was said and done, after all, her sisters already pitied her for being pregnant and alone, and Emmie had been equally quick to notice that even Kat was shy of expressing her love and affection for Mikhail in her sister's inhibiting presence. No, the unmarried pregnant sister had been wiser staying at home when she had the excuse.

To avoid such negative thoughts, Emmie had spent every spare moment researching local craftspeople to supply merchandise for the gift shop while also checking out the strict requirements for running a café. That project had kept Emmie extremely busy. Although she had little time to mope she often lay awake late into the night picturing a lean, darkly handsome face and aching unbearably as though she had lost a limb. In spite of the fact that she had found it impossible to envisage a feasible future with Bastian, walking away from him had still hurt like hell. But it would have been crazy, she reasoned, to hang around on the outskirts of Bastian's life, sleeping with him in the forlorn hope that he would eventually want to take their relationship to another level or assume a regular paternal role once the twins were born. She needed to get over him and she needed to do it fast, she told herself impatiently. And in her opinion seeing too much of Saffy's and Kat's deliriously happy marriages to the men they loved was unlikely to help her to recover from her own unrequited love any more quickly. Indeed her sisters' success and contentment on that front only made Emmie feel like a total failure in the love stakes.

For the second time in as many weeks, Bastian drove up to the Lake District. A glossy celebrity magazine lay open on the passenger seat beside him and every time he noticed it he gritted his teeth, a ferocious sense of injustice assailing him. On this occasion, Bastian needed no directions to reach his destination because he knew exactly where he was going as he nosed his Ferrari into the driveway of the farmhouse, parked it, dug the magazine into his pocket and sprang out to stride impatiently to the front door.

Emmie groaned as the doorbell buzzed because she was in the middle of making pastry and her hands were covered with flour. She wiped her hands on the front of her apron, surprised as she always was to feel the firm swell of her pregnant stomach arching out in front of her. She was the size of a small house, which, according to the local doctor, was only to be expected with twins on the way. She trundled to the front door and pulled it open, lashes fluttering up on startled blue eyes as she focused on the tall black-haired male on the doorstep.

Sheathed in a dark suit and a cashmere overcoat, Bastian surveyed her with brooding intensity, narrowed dark eyes glittering like polished jet. 'Surprise… surprise…'

CHAPTER NINE

EMMIE STEPPED BACK and Bastian stalked through the front door, slamming it shut in his wake with an imperious hand.

'I wasn't planning to invite you in,' Emmie snapped.

'Given enough rope you really will hang yourself, won't you?' Bastian riposted with derision. 'Perhaps you'd like to explain why I only qualified for one sentence of explanation when you staged your disappearing act. In fact, what exactly was "This isn't working for me" supposed to convey?'

Emmie stiffened, acknowledging that while she hadn't wanted to go emotionally overboard in her goodbye note she had perhaps tried a little too hard to play it cool. 'I don't want to discuss it.'

Bastian threw back his wide shoulders and stared down at her with blistering force, his handsome mouth a hard ruthless line. 'We're going to discuss a lot of things before I leave here, *glyka mou*.'

Emmie stared at him, unwillingly captivated by the sheer gorgeous potency of Bastian in the flesh. Radiating masculine energy and buckets of authority, Bastian towered over her, scanning her appearance in a red roll-neck sweater, apron and jeans. 'You've put on weight…'

'Duh! You noticed?' Emmie shot back at him witheringly, turning on her heel to march back towards the kitchen.

As she stood briefly sideways Bastian focused on the swell of her pregnant belly pushing out the apron and stared, taken aback by the size of her. 'I meant… you haven't lost any *more* weight, so I assume the sickness wore off—'

'Weeks ago,' Emmie confirmed, turning back to face him again with open reluctance, blonde hair tumbling round her flushed cheeks.

'And yet you didn't think to get in touch with me and tell me that?' Bastian fired back at her furiously. 'Didn't it occur to you that I'd be worried about you? When I last saw you, you were far from well!'

'I thought with you it would be a case of out of sight, out of mind,' Emmie admitted truthfully, straightening her slender shoulders and standing her ground in the kitchen doorway lest he get the idea that she was intimidated by him.

'Those babies are half mine!' Bastian launched back at her wrathfully. 'When did I ever give you the impression that I was so irresponsible?'

Emmie pretended to think deeply. 'Oh, maybe it was when you warned me not to get worked up about having sex with you…I *didn't*, by the way.'

A feverish veil of colour highlighted his spectacular

cheekbones and his dark golden eyes blazed like the heart of a hot fire. 'Maybe I was playing safe.'

'Playing safe?' Emmie queried, all at sea.

His beautiful wilful mouth hardened. *'Ne…*yes, you blow hot, you blow cold, and you run away. That's twice you've done that to me now.'

Emmie took an angry step forward. 'I do not blow hot and cold and I do *not* run away!'

'You do,' Bastian contradicted with maddening assurance. 'I offended you the night before Nessa's wedding and you went from hotter than hot to cold as charity and ran away from the attraction between us. You may be an adult but you suffer from the same emotional overreactions as a teenager!'

'How dare you?' Emmie snapped, fit to be tied at that slur being cast on her maturity.

'I dare because I'm honest and I have *always* been honest with you,' Bastian declared with impressive emphasis. 'We had a disastrous misunderstanding the very first night we were together—I apologised—you refused to accept my apology. But at least I was willing to admit that I had made a mistake but was still attracted to you. We would never have been apart had you had the courage to be equally honest with me…'

'It's not about honesty, it's about sensitivity, and you are the guy who told me that what we had was just sex!' Emmie slammed back at him emotively.

'At the end of the day, sex is only sex and I stand by that statement!' Bastian growled back at her unapologetically. 'But in every way that mattered I demonstrated that I cared about what happened to you and I cared about the welfare of those babies you carry.'

Emmie struggled to be fair while her deep sense of having been insulted still rankled. 'Yes, you did,' she allowed, tight-mouthed at having to concede that point.

'I didn't deserve that you walked out on me and didn't tell me where you were going.'

'I would have got in touch with you *after* the birth,' Emmie protested.

'I want to be a lot *more* involved than that,' Bastian informed her with unconcealed hostility.

Emmie lifted her chin, refusing to back down. 'Well, I'm sorry if you don't like it but perhaps I didn't feel that you being more involved in my pregnancy was appropriate in the circumstances.'

'If that's how you felt you should have discussed it with me,' Bastian argued fiercely. 'Walking out and vanishing the minute I was safely out of the country was childish and cowardly!'

'I wanted to avoid a big confrontation like this!' Emmie pointed out.

'How are you doing with that ambition?' Bastian derided, making her teeth grind together in frustration.

'I am not childish and I am not cowardly,' Emmie returned resentfully to his determination to blame her for walking away from a difficult relationship.

'No? Well, at the very least you have some strange hang-ups,' Bastian condemned, interrupting her without hesitation as he dug a magazine out of his pocket and slapped it down aggressively on the hall table.

'She's your sister, your twin, and presumably the reason you go around dressed in a frumpy disguise most of the time! But did you think to mention her existence to me even once?'

Emmie froze in consternation as she found herself gazing down at a magazine photo of Saffy and Zahir's wedding day. Laughing and smiling with happiness, Saffy looked fantastic and Emmie's heart constricted at the sight, regret belatedly stabbing her that she had avoided playing a role at her sister's nuptials. 'How did you find out?'

'Nessa saw it and put it in front of me. I couldn't believe what I was seeing,' Bastian admitted with angry dark eyes. 'At first I thought it was you marrying royalty and then I saw her name…she's Sapphire, you're Emerald, so it was obviously no coincidental likeness. I did some research and that's when I realised how much you had been hiding from me.'

'There was no need for you to know.'

'I couldn't believe *she* was your sister.'

Emmie lost colour at that admission. 'I understand that. We may be identical twins but she still looks very different from me.'

'Yes, even though it was only photos I was merely fooled into thinking it was you for about five seconds,' Bastian spelt out.

Unsurprised by the assertion but dreading the comparison he had to be making between her and her gorgeous sister, Emmie lowered her head, her face shadowing. 'Yes—'

'You have a beauty spot on one cheekbone and your eyes are a lighter blue,' Bastian contended, sharply disconcerting her for few people were that observant. 'I also suspect that you're smaller—'

'By at least an inch. Even after the surgery on my leg I never quite caught up with Saffy in height,' Emmie conceded. 'I don't wear a disguise though—you don't understand…I just don't like being mistaken for Saffy and, believe me, it happens a lot if I dress up and go out and about in London. She's a celebrity, after all. I've also found it's just easier not to mention that she's my sister to the people I meet.'

'I can imagine that but you're not the same—you're not carbon copies of each other.'

'You don't think so?'

'I don't quite understand it but when I look at her, she does as much for my libido as a blank canvas on the wall, but when I look at you I have an instant reaction,' Bastian confessed in a husky undertone.

Emmie wasn't quite sure she could believe that, for she was much more accustomed to thinking of her sister as a vastly superior, more sophisticated and sexier version of herself—in every way a supermodel-perfect creature. But then Saffy had always been the prettier, livelier, more talented twin, Emmie the sickly, shy one, who was boringly academic, not that she had had much choice on that score when her disability had meant she couldn't go out and about like her twin. She glanced up at Bastian, her lovely face pink with self-consciousness, wondering if it could possibly be true that he found her more sexually appealing than her sister. After all, all her life she had been second-best to Saffy.

'It happens *every* time I look at you,' Bastian imparted thickly, his dark deep drawl vibrating down her spine, his stunning dark golden eyes hotly pinned to her in a smouldering look that created an atmosphere of shocking intimacy. 'Because while I know it's just sex, it's still the most freakin' fantastic sex I've ever had with a woman!'

A surge of responsive heat flooded Emmie's pelvis, swelled her breasts, tightened her nipples and no matter how hard she tried she couldn't suppress that wave of physical awareness. Bastian was attempting to turn an insult into a compliment and failing abysmally, she told herself firmly. She wasn't going to pick him up on it; she wasn't going to go there at all. Talking about sex with Bastian was a bad idea because talking about it made her think about it and she was determined to keep the door closed on that kind of misleading intimacy.

Breathing in deep, she turned her head away to duck his direct gaze and said tautly, 'So how did you find out where I was living?'

'Once I had linked you to your celebrity sister I had enquiries made and discovered this place,' Bastian told her, his handsome mouth compressing with annoyance. 'I drove up here straight away but you weren't here and the house was locked up.'

'Oh…' Emmie was surprised he had come to the farmhouse on a previous occasion and couldn't hide it.

'Did you come here at the weekend? I must have been staying with Kat.'

Bastian was frowning down at her. 'Your eldest sister? The one married to the rich Russian, who owns this house?'

Emmie studied him in surprise at the level of his knowledge. 'You have been doing your homework about my family.'

'Enough to know that you shouldn't be living here, forced to rely on the generosity of another man.'

'That other man happens to be my brother-in-law—'

'It doesn't matter. You're in this situation because of me and I'm the one who should be taking care of you.'

Emmie threw her head high, her lovely face taut with strain as she shifted her weight onto her one leg while rubbing at the thigh of the other. 'I don't need anyone taking care of me when I can do that for myself.'

'But I *want* to do it,' Bastian grated in a raw undertone, watching her massage her leg. 'Your leg's hurting you right now. Why don't you sit down? I want to look after the mother of my children. Is that so wrong?'

Emmie was disconcerted by that blunt declaration and that he had actually noticed that her leg was beginning to bother her. 'No, not wrong, but maybe a little surprising after some of the things you've said.'

'Why don't you forget what I've said in the past and look to the future instead? I think right now that would be a lot more useful,' Bastian countered with ringing confidence, striding into the cosy living room where a log fire had burned low in the grate.

Emmie followed him at a slower pace. 'What future?'

'Yours and the twins',' Bastian specified, gazing back at her with challenging intensity. 'I want you to come back to Greece with me and meet my family.'

Her eyes widened in astonishment. 'Er…I've already met your family,' she protested.

'Not as the future mother of my kids. You can't keep us in the closet with two babies on the way,' Bastian informed her with dark eyes glittering with amusement. 'You're part of my life now and that's not going to change.'

'I still don't think that there's any need for you to take me back to Greece with you and make some sort of formal announcement,' Emmie contended.

'I think it's important.' Bastian's stubborn jawline clenched his face taut as he stared back at her. 'Family connections mean a great deal to me. It'll be easier for you to make that connection now *before* the twins are born.'

'I'm not interested in visiting Greece right now,' Emmie declared, throwing her shoulders back.

'I want the time to see if we can work this relationship out,' Bastian admitted in a driven undertone. 'I shouldn't have to spell that out to you.'

Her troubled eyes widened a little and remained glued to his stunning dark eyes as if she was seeking answers there. 'Oh, I think you do…speaking as the guy who told me that all we had going for us was sex.'

'Are you ever going to let me forget I said that?' Bastian slammed back at her furiously.

'Probably not,' Emmie admitted waspishly. 'It's still screaming in my memory banks. Now all of a sudden you've changed your tune and you're talking about us working out this relationship when before you wouldn't even admit we *had* a relationship!'

In thunderous silence Bastian ground his teeth together. Like salt on an open wound she picked up every mistake he made and flung it at him with an aggression he was unaccustomed to meeting with in a woman. 'So I'm not perfect,' he bit out grudgingly.

'And you have hang-ups too,' Emmie added sweetly. 'Particularly when it comes to commitment.'

'I was engaged,' Bastian reminded her darkly.

'But funnily enough you never made it to the altar,' Emmie remarked.

'Lilah took offence at the pre-nuptial contract she was presented with and I wouldn't marry her without it.'

'I don't *want* your money,' Emmie told him baldly.

Bastian flattened his passionate mouth into a hard line and lowered his attention to her stomach. 'But your children will be entitled to a good deal of my money. That's a fact of life.'

Emmie coloured uncomfortably, not knowing what to say to that that wouldn't sound facetious, for in all likelihood when the babies she carried grew up they *would* want and expect access to their father's privileged lifestyle.

'I'll stay here tonight. We'll leave in the morning,' Bastian told her forcefully.

'You can't just bully me into travelling to Greece with you!' Emmie exclaimed, not knowing whether to laugh or cry at his attitude.

'I'm not trying to bully you. I'm asking you to put the needs of our children first. At the very least we need to establish a more civilised connection.'

There was a lot of truth in that statement, Emmie acknowledged uneasily. Having a contentious relationship with the father of her children was a very bad idea but she did not know if she could change the way she felt about Bastian or forgive him for not feeling the same way about her. She wanted too much and he wanted too little, she conceded unhappily.

'All right, I'll think about Greece,' Emmie muttered tightly.

'I'll make the arrangements—'

'Look, when the heck did "I'll think about it" turn into agreement?' Emmie stormed back at him, out of all patience with his arrogance.

Bastian stared broodingly back at her, the full intensity of his aggressive temperament in that charged appraisal. Electric heat sizzled through Emmie and she flushed, mortified by the way he affected her even when he was demonstrating his least attractive traits. On the other hand maybe if she gave a little, he would as well, because she didn't think that with the twins on the way it was wise to be at odds with him. After all, mightn't her attitude have a bad effect on his future relationship with her children? That, she acknowledged hollowly, was a major responsibility to carry, particularly when she was all too well aware how wounding she had found her own father's indifference to her existence. She definitely didn't want her children to undergo the same paternal rejection because she had created a problematic relationship with Bastian. Hadn't her mother done that with her father? Her parents had had a very bitter breakup and divorce and that reality had poisoned her father's attitude to his daughters as well. He had found it easier to walk away from *all* of them, not only his ex-wife.

'OK, I'll go to Greece,' Emmie agreed abruptly on the back of that final depressing thought. 'I'll show you up to your room.'

His room, *not* hers. Bastian watched the ripe curve of Emmie's hips going up the stairs, unwillingly allowing that his hopes of an immediate dropping of all barriers had been rather too optimistic. She wanted him to work at things, relationship things, and Bastian had never worked at anything like that in his whole life. Women had always worked to please him, to fit *his* expectations, not the other way round. He gritted his even white teeth at what seemed like a memory from the far distant past for he could see that pleasing him was not even on Emmie's agenda. It bothered him that he didn't even know what she wanted from him. He was doing his best but so far he had not got any points for trying, he reflected angrily. She hadn't noticed one blasted positive thing he had done so far, so why was he bothering? The answer to that question came fast: he didn't *know*, he just knew he couldn't leave her alone.

Emmie showed Bastian into one of the guest rooms her sister Kat had always kept prepared for guests. She studied his bold bronzed profile from below her lashes, reckoning there was no escape from feeding him as well while wondering why he brought out such a mean streak in her. Did she want him to go hungry? After all, it wasn't his fault that he hadn't fallen madly in love with her, was it? That was something that either happened or didn't happen. And unlike her estranged father, Bastian was already determined to make a major effort to be a parent from the start, well, before the twins were even born.

'There's hot water if you want a shower,' Emmie told him, belatedly wondering if she was trying to be hostess of the year a little too late. 'You can join me for dinner in an hour. It'll be a change to have company. My younger sister is only here for school holidays. She stays with Kat and Mikhail in London now if she leaves school to come home for the weekend.'

Bastian supposed she was offering him an olive branch of sorts and had a sudden recollection of that written apology on her hand way back at the start of their acquaintance. He almost smiled but the strained look in her bright blue eyes made him tense up instead.

* * *

'What did you say?' Emmie prompted Bastian in a nervous whisper, her cheeks burning after he had finished addressing his household staff, who had assembled in the big hall to greet their arrival. The official line-up struck her as incredibly Edwardian in style and thoroughly intimidated her. To be fair, she thought unhappily, it was embarrassing enough to reappear on the island on Bastian's arm while toting an enormous pregnant stomach, but it was even worse when absolutely everyone else was pointedly avoiding looking in that direction.

'Why?' Bastian asked shortly as he guided her up the main staircase with a firm hand at her back. Emmie wondered if he feared that she was so big upfront that she might over-balance and fall over backwards like a beached whale, and then scolded herself for being so self-critical. *You're very pregnant with twins, get over it,* she told herself in exasperation.

'I'm curious,' Emmie admitted.

'I told them that you're in charge here now—'

'You did…*what*?' Emmie stopped dead to exclaim in astonishment.

Bastian frowned. 'I didn't want anyone wondering about what your status was here and I want you to receive the very best attention possible from my staff.'

'But I'm not the mistress here…or wife or whatever!' Emmie argued.

'Do we need a label for you? To all intents and purposes you are the most important woman I've ever had in my life,' Bastian countered. 'You're expecting my children.'

'I can't possibly be the *most* important woman…I mean, what about your mother?'

'Apart from the fact that I'd have a problem if she was still the most important woman at my age,' Bastian quipped, 'what about her?'

'Is she still alive?'

'Yes. She lives in Italy and I only see her if she wants money.'

Emmie's brow furrowed. 'That's sad, Bastian. Are you sure you're not misjudging her?'

'Remind yourself of what your mother was willing to do to you in the name of profit,' Bastian commented with considerable cynicism. 'As the son of a woman even more mercenary than Odette, I know what I'm talking about.'

That reminder about Odette's greed struck home but Emmie gave him a troubled look, dismayed by his outlook. 'Why do you think your mother's like that?'

Bastian sighed as he threw wide the door of the room where Emmie had stayed on her previous visit to his home. 'Why are you interested?'

Emmie thought fast and hard, desperate to come up with an unemotional angle to conceal her revealing hunger for every detail she could glean about Bastian and his background. 'Your mother will be my children's grandmother.'

'But Cinzia will never visit your children. Even when I was a little boy she found the idea of being seen with a child as "too aging",' he retorted drily. 'She's very vain and will never accept being a grandparent. She was a film star when my father met her but her earning power was fading because she was getting older. She married him because she needed a meal ticket and when she got tired of him, she divorced him in a process that took half of everything he possessed.'

Emmie winced as a servant settled her cases down in the beautifully appointed bedroom and withdrew. 'Nasty.'

'His ego battered, my father found comfort in the arms of his secretary instead,' Bastian continued even more drily. 'The secretary got pregnant and he married her within weeks of his divorce from my mother being granted.'

'Oh dear,' Emmie remarked a good deal less securely as she wondered if he saw a dangerous parallel in that development between past and present: his father had married a woman because she fell pregnant by him and clearly it hadn't worked out.

'She was Nessa's mother and the only decent woman my father ever married,' Bastian explained wryly. 'But because my father wasn't in *love* with her...' contempt edged his tone as he voiced that particular word '...he thought it was acceptable to start an affair with the woman who became his third wife.'

'Then I gather that Nessa's mother didn't last long?'

'Two years.'

Emmie recalled Nessa telling her that her mother had been the only stepmother who was kind to Bastian and, considering his own mother had not set a good example of maternal affection, she found it sad that his father's marriage to Nessa's mother had been so brief. 'And wife number three?'

'Had one affair after another. My father hit the bottle hard before he finally got shot of her.'

'He sounds—'

'Foolish?' Bastian scorned.

'I was going to say vulnerable. I mean, he kept on trying so hard to find a happy relationship.'

'Only the grass on the other side of the fence was always greener and he couldn't content himself,' Bastian completed grimly. 'Wife number four spent most of her time trying to get *me* into bed because younger men gave her a buzz.'

That revelation made Emmie turn pink. 'That must have been ghastly.'

'While that marriage went on, I spent a lot of time at my grandfather's house—I was only eighteen,' Bastian admitted flatly, staring out of the bedroom window, broad shoulders rigid. 'Tragically my father's fourth marriage literally killed him. He came home unexpectedly one day and overheard his wife trying to seduce me. He got back into his car and crashed it into a tree a few miles down the road. The happy widow got what was left of my father's estate, which wasn't much. His marriages had virtually bankrupted him.'

'With a family history like that I'm surprised you were even considering getting married,' Emmie confided truthfully.

Bastian turned away from the window, tall, darkly handsome and intensely charismatic. His dark eyes glittered like gleaming gold ingots in sunlight. 'But unlike my father I didn't have any stupid ideas about love having anything to do with marriage…'

Emmie was relieved to think that Bastian had not been in love with Lilah, but his words and his attitude certainly didn't offer *her* much room for hope that he might develop such feelings for her in the future. 'Have you ever been in love?' she asked baldly, reasoning that subtlety was wasted on Bastian.

'In lust many times,' Bastian quipped. 'In love… never. I'm probably too practical.'

So, at the very least he must have been in lust with Lilah, Emmie assumed uneasily, and she certainly couldn't blame him for that because his ex-fiancée was exquisitely easy on the eye. 'I fell in love when I was at university,' she heard herself admit.

Unaccustomed to such personal conversations with a woman, Bastian dealt her a disconcerted look.

Emmie compressed her lush mouth. 'It turned out that Toby was only with me because he had a poster of my sister the supermodel on his bedroom wall—she was his fantasy and I was just the closest he could get to her,' she related ruefully.

'What a fool when you're even more beautiful,' Bastian breathed huskily.

'I'm not more beautiful than Saffy,' Emmie protested.

'I think you are,' Bastian admitted, his dark gaze

roaming over her lovely face. 'You're more natural, not all made up and artificial like your sibling.'

Without warning and for the first time in her life, Emmie found herself laughing at a comparison being made that could not leave her feeling inadequate. 'Well, I'm certainly not anywhere near as well groomed as my sister,' she conceded with a smile. 'She always looks perfect.'

Bastian rested lean brown hands on her slim shoulders, gazing down at her with smouldering heat in his heavily fringed dark golden eyes. 'I don't want or need perfect, *khriso mou.*'

Emmie stiffened, suddenly unsure of what should happen next, wanting him with every skin cell in her treacherous body but conscious that intimacy would plunge her deeper into a relationship that had no safe boundaries to protect her from hurt. 'Bastian…er—'

Long brown fingers brushed her cheekbone in a lazy caress and he kissed her with hungry driving urgency. Her heart hammered so fast she was scared it would burst out of her chest. The glorious swell of emotion and sensation that only he could give her was waiting in the wings like a terrible temptation, making nonsense of her firm conviction that she could take care of herself. For a split second she wanted Bastian so much it was terrifying, her body kindling like dry twigs touched by a flame, senses awakening with a surge of slumberous intensity. Her breasts stirred beneath her clothing, full and swollen and ripe for his touch, an ache biting deep in her pelvis to leave a sense of hollowness in its wake.

'I should unpack,' she said breathlessly, drawing back in a movement that demanded every atom of her self-discipline while her glance briefly skimmed over the door that led into Bastian's bedroom, and she wondered how long she could possibly keep her distance from him.

In a rare act for a male in the grip of fierce arousal, Bastian backed off several steps, lean, strong face taut and flushed. Emmie was in Greece, on the island of Treikos, safely beneath his roof, and that was enough for one day, he reflected ruefully, apprehensive for the first time ever of making a wrong move with a woman.

Conscious of the tension in the air, Emmie coloured and turned aside to her luggage. Her legs were shaking, her rebellious body screaming with tight, strained nerve endings and she was ashamed of her weakness. Somehow it had not occurred to her that Bastian might still exert that much physical power over her even when she was several months pregnant. Where he was concerned, she badly needed an off switch.

Four days later, Nessa arrived for the weekend and mortified Emmie straight away by walking out to the terrace where Emmie and Bastian were having lunch and saying cheerfully, 'So, when's the wedding?'

Bastian frowned. 'What wedding?' he queried, standing up to pull out a chair for his sister.

Nessa simply laughed. '*Your* wedding, of course,'

she said teasingly, studying the pair of them with amused brown eyes.

'We're not getting married,' Emmie declared with red cheeks hot enough to fry eggs on.

Nessa raised a brow as though that was an extraordinary statement and responded, 'Grandpa is going to be very disappointed.'

Initially relieved by Nessa's arrival because the presence of a third person would surely stifle the shocking level of sexual tension Bastian roused inside her, Emmie could now only feel appalled at the brunette's lack of tact.

'I don't think so,' Bastian countered smoothly, seemingly unembarrassed, Emmie noted with some relief.

'Trust me.' Nessa grinned. 'Grandpa's expecting to hear wedding bells and just waiting on you making the announcement. Don't say you weren't warned.'

'Excuse me,' Emmie breathed, rising to her feet.

'Where are you going?' Bastian demanded as if he was entitled to know her every move.

'It's hot and I'm a little tired…thought I'd lie down for a while,' Emmie told him disjointedly, taking refuge in being pregnant in her eagerness to escape sitting in on a humiliating dialogue between brother and sister.

Upstairs she lay down on her bed, dully recalling what entertaining company Bastian had been since their arrival. They had picnicked on the beach, wandered through olive groves on lazy walks and eaten in the taverna down by the harbour where Emmie had suspected that all the other diners were staring at her.

Even so, apart from that one kiss on the first day, Bastian hadn't touched her again. She was never going to understand Bastian, she reflected in frustration. Why had he kissed her if he had no plans to follow up on it? And *why*, when she knew that intimacy would only fire them into dangerous territory again, was she even wondering?

Her cell phone pinged on a message and she snatched it up, surprised to see that it was from Saffy, who rarely made direct contact with her.

'I'm in the pudding club too,' Saffy texted jokily, and Emmie gasped and before she could even consider what she was doing she was phoning her twin. It struck her as extraordinary that both of them should contrive to be pregnant at the same time.

Saffy was audibly disconcerted to hear Emmie's voice on the line but the warmth of her response soothed any awkwardness Emmie might have felt. When Saffy startled Emmie by freely admitting that she had conceived her baby *before* marrying Zahir, Emmie was captivated and touched by her honesty and the barriers really came down between the sisters as Emmie shared the history of her relationship with Bastian.

At one point, Saffy interrupted her twin. 'Odette lied to you. She *didn't* pay for your surgery, Kat did!'

'Are you sure? But where did Kat get the money from?' Emmie questioned in amazement.

'Kat took out a loan to cover the cost. Our mother is a dreadful liar.' Saffy groaned. 'As for this escort agency stuff, we'll have to prevent Topsy from visiting her or she'll be trying to set her up next! Topsy's *so* trusting and I bet Odette milked our kid sister for every bit of useful info about us that she could get.'

'Probably,' Emmie conceded, shocked at the news that her mother had deceived her but at the same time semi-stunned that she was managing to have such a friendly conversation with her twin when they had been estranged for so long. 'I'm sorry I didn't come to your wedding, Saffy. It's no excuse but I was feeling pretty down and I just couldn't face it.'

'I'll forgive you if you promise…to stay in touch with me,' her sister responded hesitantly.

Her heart lifting at that request, Emmie was quick to agree.

'You said you were in Greece—what's happening between you and Bastian right now?' Saffy finally asked.

'I think that for the sake of the future, we're trying to be friends,' Emmie told her heavily.

'And you want more?' Saffy asked perceptively. 'I felt the same way with Zahir. I didn't want him to stay with me only because I was pregnant.'

Emmie's eyes stung at the depth of her twin's understanding. She blinked back tears and a little while after that the groundbreaking conversation concluded with Saffy promising to phone again the next day. Afterwards, Emmie sat still dumbfounded by the discovery that she could talk easily again to her twin and she was so grateful that neither of them had dared to broach any topic that might be controversial. That both sisters were pregnant, however, had provided them with a bridge that spanned the challenges of their shared past. In addition, Emmie acknowledged wryly, Bastian had somehow contrived to lift Emmie's confidence so that she no longer felt that she was a poor, disappointing copy of her glamorous and vibrant twin.

'You should invite Saffy and her husband to visit,' Bastian remarked when she volunteered the news over dinner that she and her sister were talking again. Nessa had gone to visit her in-laws, who lived in the village.

Emmie tensed. 'That's very kind of you but obviously I don't know how long I'll be staying here in your home.'

Bastian raised an ebony brow, brilliant dark eyes bright as diamonds in his handsome face. 'At least until the twins are born,' he supplied without hesitation. 'I want you to stay, and when I return to London to work, I'll want you to accompany me there as well.'

Taken aback by that sweeping statement, Emmie studied him with shaken blue eyes. 'I had no idea that's what you were planning. I thought I was only here for a short visit.'

Across the table, Bastian stared steadily back at her. 'Naturally you're free to do whatever you want and live where you choose…but speaking on my own behalf *I* want you to *stay* with me.'

Emmie was hugely touched by that assurance even though she still had no real idea of what he meant by his words. Did he believe that simply being pregnant was so hazardous that he had to keep a careful watch over her? Did he feel guilty that he had got her pregnant? Was that why he was so determined to look after her? Or was there a more personal element than that? As she bent over her delicious dessert, she was insanely conscious of his attention locking to the rather low neckline of her top. She glanced up quickly and tracked the path of his hot golden gaze locked to the plump swell of her cleavage. She reddened and thought, *Yes, it's definitely personal.*

'Does that invite of yours include sharing a bed?' Emmie enquired baldly.

A sudden grin flashed across Bastian's stubborn mouth. 'I'm yours any time you want me, *khriso mou.* I don't play hard to get.'

Emmie didn't know where to look because when she met his stunning eyes after that admission she felt intoxicated and dizzy. Unable to think straight, she savoured the sweetness of her dessert, the tip of her tongue sliding out to lick a drop of chocolate mousse from her full bottom lip.

Following that process, his attention locked to her succulent pink mouth, Bastian groaned out loud. 'You're killing me.'

Emmie froze. In the condition she was in she found it quite impossible to view herself as seductive in any way, but when she looked across the table to see Bastian's molten golden gaze welded to her, her heart skipped a startled beat. He thrust back his chair and sprang upright, approaching her to stretch down a lean brown hand and grasp hers to tug her to her feet.

'Bastian…?' Emmie framed uncertainly.

'I want you so much,' he growled. 'I've been working so hard to keep my hands off you.'

Emmie had only felt her own tension and had not appreciated that he was exercising restraint as well. 'You find me attractive like this?' she murmured wonderingly.

Bastian looked down at her with smouldering dark eyes. 'I don't really understand it but I find your pregnancy an amazing turn-on.'

'OK,' Emmie marvelled while nodding dumbly, entranced by the hunger etched in his face and the very slight yet revealing tremor in his hands as he raised them to gently cup her cheekbones.

And then there was no more talking and the last barrier crashed down between them while he kissed her breathless. He took her upstairs to lift her into his bed, where he made slow sensual love to her until she cried out her pleasure in wondering wanton delight.

A long time later, he lay with his arms wrapped round her and the most glorious sense of peace settled over Emmie. She loved it when he held her close and wanted to swarm all over his long, lean, powerful body like a flock of bees savouring pollen. Self-discipline, however, kept her still and unadventurous because she was terrified of revealing too much emotion or enthusiasm. Sex was sex, as Bastian had told her unforgettably, and she didn't want to begin kidding herself that it was anything more. While they were living together, they might as well be sharing a bed, she bargained desperately with herself. She didn't have to have a relationship all set out in stone steps in front of her to be happy, did she? And why shouldn't she settle for being happy for now and letting the future take care of itself?

'I have a charity ball to attend in Athens tomorrow evening,' Bastian told her when she had almost drifted to sleep. 'You're welcome to accompany me.'

'Nothing to wear, *truly* nothing to wear!' Emmie exclaimed, eyes flying wide in dismay in the darkness. 'But thanks for asking…er, appearing in public this pregnant with you would be kind of making a really loud statement, wouldn't it?'

'It would,' Bastian agreed with a curious lack of expression. 'Perhaps you're right and it's too soon.'

Emmie hadn't said or meant that but she didn't argue, reasoning that he would have tried harder to persuade her to go with him if her presence had really mattered to him. Thirty-six hours later those same thoughts came home to haunt her with a vengeance.

The morning after the Athens ball, Bastian had still to return to the island and Emmie was having a leisurely breakfast on the terrace overlooking the beach when the morning newspapers were brought out and settled on a nearby table for her convenience. Emmie got up to browse through the pile of papers, automatically flipping past the Greek editions only for her fingers to falter as she stiffened in consternation at the sight of a photograph adorning the front page of one of the local tabloids.

It was a photo of Bastian and Lilah drinking champagne and laughing together. Lilah looked tiny and ravishing in a romantic pink chiffon gown, like one half of a matched couple on intimate and friendly terms, while Bastian smiled down at her. The bitter hurt of jealousy pierced Emmie deep. In fact Emmie felt as sick as though she had been punched because she was already recalling that Bastian really hadn't made that much effort to persuade her that he wanted her with him in Athens. And was this why? Had he known beforehand that Lilah would be attending the same event? And was it any wonder that the papers were probably speculating as to whether or not the formerly engaged couple had reconciled?

Feeling shaken, scared and angry with herself for being scared, Emmie sank back down on her chair, eyes blank as she stared out unseeingly at the beautiful view she had been admiring only minutes earlier. Was Bastian still attracted to Lilah? To be fair, what man wouldn't be? And what could Emmie possibly do about it, if he was? Retreating with dignity when she was already virtually living with Bastian would be a challenge in the circumstances, she thought painfully.

CHAPTER TEN

EMMIE WAS CONVINCED that she could only blame herself for her predicament. Clearly, it was all her *own* fault, an argument her mother had been prone to making every time anything went wrong in Emmie's life when she was a child.

Here she was, after all, decidedly the author of her own destruction: pregnant and having an affair with Bastian in a relationship that had neither rules nor safe boundaries. How sensible was that? Emmie had always liked to know where she stood, only she never had known that when it came to Bastian. That was why she was reluctant to trust him and even more reluctant to risk relying on him. And there would soon be no room for self-respect either if she was forced to start questioning him about Lilah.

The helicopter flew in low and fast and began to land. Emmie didn't move a muscle. She did try to cross her legs casually beneath her white cotton sundress but her large tummy got in the way and she had to forget that pose. Bastian leapt from the helicopter into view, black hair ruffled by the breeze, lean powerful body taut as he strode across the lawn to join her, his striking black-fringed dark golden eyes seeking Emmie out where she sat in the shade. As always, he was gorgeous, she conceded helplessly. She had only to look at his tense bone structure to guess that he knew about the photograph and was in an understandably wary frame of mind.

'You look so serene and beautiful sitting there, *khriso mou*,' Bastian imparted huskily, his attention lingering to take in the rich golden gleam of her hair and the glow of her delicate English-rose complexion in contrast to her bright blue eyes.

'Appearances can be deceptive,' Emmie quipped.

'I flew straight back when I saw that photo…I gather you've seen it?' An ebony brow quirked enquiringly.

Emmie nodded, reluctantly impressed that he had jumped right into the issue without trying to avoid it or fake an innocence that she would never have believed.

'Aside of the fact that Nessa was with me throughout the evening, the photo was a definite stitch-up,' Bastian complained with a sardonic look. 'Probably set up by Lilah and taken by one of her friends. Lilah revels in provoking press attention and speculation.'

Emmie parted stiff lips, her hands clasped together tightly below the level of the table. 'You do look happy to be with her,' she remarked flatly.

'After the way Lilah behaved when we broke up I no longer even like her,' Bastian countered drily. 'But I have too much respect for her family to cut her dead in public and I see no reason to embarrass myself or her by parading our differences. If I'm happy now it's because I have *you* in my life.'

'I'd never have guessed I mattered that much to you,' Emmie confided uncomfortably, sitting very still and unconvinced, her shoulders as rigid as her spine.

A rueful smile briefly curled Bastian's wide sensual mouth. 'I'm so terrified of losing you again you wouldn't believe it.'

Emmie blinked. 'I don't believe it…you, *terrified*?'

'Totally,' Bastian confirmed, staring down at her from his considerable height with steady, dark, serious eyes. 'When you went missing while I was still abroad I went crazy. I couldn't eat, I couldn't sleep, I couldn't think of anything but you. And when I did get back to London I couldn't believe that stupid note you left was all you had to say to me.'

'I didn't think I had anything to say to you that you had enough interest to want to hear,' Emmie admitted uneasily. 'I wasn't going to hang myself out on a limb for you after you said that all we had going for us was sex.'

'I didn't mean that…I very much *regret* saying that,' Bastian emphasised on the back of a groan. 'But to be frank, I didn't really appreciate what you meant to me until you vanished.'

'Oh?' Emmie was glued to every word falling from his lips, scarcely breathing while she listened.

Bastian leant back against one of the supporting stone pillars that held up the roof over the terrace, his gaze veiled, his lean muscular length taut with tension. 'Then I didn't feel anything like I should have felt for Lilah. I know that now. I shouldn't have even considered marrying her when I felt nothing for her, but for a long time I honestly thought that that was the best way to be in a relationship.'

'If you're an inanimate object and not a person,' Emmie suggested wryly.

'I thought if there was no emotion involved I would see more clearly and choose a wife more wisely,' Bastian confessed and then frowned, black brows lacing together. 'And we know how well that turned out! Lilah may have wanted me mainly for my status and wealth but even she deserved better than a fiancé who couldn't have cared less when she broke the engagement and took up with another man.'

'But she must have known that it was more a...er practical marriage than a meeting of souls,' Emmie commented tightly, thinking what a hypocrite she could be, for she had been wonderfully reassured by Bastian's assurance that he didn't even like Lilah any more and it was obvious that he could no longer see what virtues he had once assumed the other woman possessed.

'I was never really happy with her...I didn't stop noticing other women either,' Bastian admitted reluctantly. 'I didn't *do* anything about it, I was faithful while I was still with her but I imagine that I would have strayed eventually.'

'Then you weren't right for each other.' Emmie

sighed. 'What would have been the point of getting married?'

'Exactly,' Bastian agreed, shooting her a smouldering smile. 'I'm so different with you. I don't like other men looking at you and I certainly have no desire to look at other women. I can't stand not knowing where you are and what you're doing. I want to be sure you'll answer your phone when I call. I want to know you're living in my home and that you'll raise our children there with me. I also want to know that you're truly *mine*.'

'Yours?' Emmie questioned. 'In what way do you want me to be yours?'

'In the most basic way that a man and a woman can belong to each other,' Bastian retorted, digging into his pocket to produce something, which he extended.

Emmie blinked at the spectacle of the huge diamond solitaire ring that he was offering her. 'Er... what's this?'

'You're bright enough to work it out,' Bastian teased. 'But it's going to be the shortest engagement on record because I intend to add a wedding ring to your finger as soon as possible.'

Emmie stiffened, facial muscles setting tight. 'I don't want you to feel you *have* to marry me because it's what your family expect of you,' she told him squarely.

'I knew they'd stick their oar in if they could but this has nothing to do with my family. This,' Bastian declared, lifting her slender hand to thread the diamond ring onto her engagement finger, 'is all about me and you and how I feel about you. I can't stand you being away from me.'

'Maybe you're just possessive,' Emmie remarked.

'I can't sleep when you're not there.'

'It's sex you miss,' Emmie contended heavily, refusing to be convinced by his transformation.

Bastian swore under his breath and lifted her up to face him. 'Stop being grumpy and difficult,' he instructed. 'Somehow I fell madly in love with you and now you've become so much a part of my life that I can't imagine it without you. It's got nothing to do with you being pregnant either—that's simply a wonderful added extra.'

'An added extra?' Emmie repeated in astonishment.

'I love you,' Bastian murmured intently, dark golden eyes locked strongly to hers. 'And I finally understand how much that emotion can enrich my life.'

'But you only hired me as an escort,' Emmie protested. 'If it hadn't been me, it would have been someone else.'

'No. You were never an escort and I've never been with one and now I never ever will be, *khriso mou*,' Bastian declared emotively. 'You were special and you dug your way into my heart and taught me to feel stuff I never thought I would or could experience.'

A great bubble of happiness was swelling inside Emmie and making her feel light-headed. 'Seriously?' she pressed.

'Seriously,' Bastian confirmed levelly.

'Pride comes before a fall,' Emmie teased with a huge grin.

'Slow and steady wins the race,' Bastian muttered, nuzzling his passionate mouth against her throat so that she shivered in the circle of his arms. 'But I'm sorry I was such a slow learner.'

'I'll forgive you because I love you too,' she whispered. 'But I didn't admit it to myself until it was almost too late because I was scared of getting too involved with you and getting hurt.'

'I will never hurt you,' Bastian swore huskily. 'My ambition is to marry you and spend my life ensuring that you and our children are happy.'

Emmie linked her arms round his neck and gazed up at him with adoring eyes and a sunny smile. 'I'm not going to complain about that. You're going to be a fantastic father as well,' she assured him with loving confidence.

'Even though I've got no manners?'

'Says the guy who opens doors for me all the time?' Emmie riposted as he did exactly that with the door in front of them.

'So you actually noticed that change in my behaviour?' Bastian quipped. 'Why didn't you mention it then?'

'Didn't want to give you a swollen head!' She gasped, breathless with excitement as he paused to kiss her.

'You have to notice to encourage me, *khriso mou*,' Bastian informed her raggedly, holding her tightly to him, ensuring that she was fully aware of the effect she was having on him.

'My word, Bastian, the last thing you need from me is encouragement!' Emmie laughed at the idea, joy sparkling through her as she wrapped her arms round him and clung to stay upright.

EPILOGUE

FOUR YEARS LATER on her wedding anniversary, Emmie strolled down to the beach where Bastian was playing ball with their toddler sons, Dmitri and Stavros, Saffy's husband, Zahir, and their son, Karim. In Emmie's arms snuggled her baby daughter, Appollonia, cute as a button at six months old with her mother's hair and her father's eyes.

For a pleasant change the usually empty stretch of beach below the house was downright crowded. Bastian's grandfather, Theron, was sharing one of the tables on the sand with Nessa, Leonides and their infant daughter, Olympia. A family BBQ was organised for later that evening. Kat and Mikhail, Topsy and their twins were due to arrive on Mikhail's fabulous yacht before nightfall. Emmie knew it would be a fantastic, noisy celebration with kids running wild and sisters talking nineteen to the dozen to catch up on the latest news and she could hardly wait.

'Give me that beautiful baby,' Saffy urged, reaching for Appollonia, who gave her aunt a gummy smile.

'Trust you to get it right. I'm having another boy when I was convinced I was carrying a little girl this time,' she lamented, patting the rounded contours of her stomach.

'Maybe the next time,' Emmie said with a grin.

'I told Zahir there wasn't going to be a next time.'

'You said that after Karim's birth as well,' Emmie reminded her twin, loving the closeness of the bond reborn after their long estrangement from each other.

'Did I?' Saffy sighed. 'Zahir is mad about kids, almost as bad as Bastian.'

A black-haired squirming bundle of lively toddler tucked under each muscular arm, Bastian lowered his twin sons to the ground and doled out cold drinks from the cool box.

Bastian strode across the sand to lift his daughter out of Saffy's arms and hold her high above him. The baby chuckled like mad, arms and plump little legs waving in frantic excitement. She was a cheerful baby with a wonderfully infectious laugh while her brothers were live-wire kids, who kept both parents on their toes.

Sometimes, Emmie could barely believe that years had passed since their quiet wedding on the island, which had only been attended by family. They had held a terrific party afterwards and just six weeks later their twin boys had been born early. One of their devoted nannies retrieved Appollonia from her father and Bastian crossed the sand to close an arm round Emmie's slim shoulders.

'Happy anniversary, *pethi mou*,' he husked, brushing his sensual mouth gently across her temples.

In the sunlight, Emmie touched the perfectly matched pearls that gleamed at her throat with appreciative fingertips, Bastian's gift to mark the occasion. As a wedding present he had given her an outrageously extravagant sapphire necklace, confiding that the first time he had watched her walking down the stairs in his island home he had pictured her sporting sapphires that matched her eyes. Her husband's generosity had ensured that her jewellery collection and her wardrobe were pretty special. Never again would Emmie be able to use the excuse that she had nothing suitable to wear, for she owned a wonderful selection of clothes. Indeed anything she wanted, Bastian ensured she received and Emmie loved being spoilt and valued for the first time in her life.

'Happy anniversary, my love,' Emmie whispered, gazing up at her darkly handsome husband with smiling warmth and love. 'Has marriage lived up to your expectations?'

Bastian tugged her close to his big sun-warmed body. 'Life with you has exceeded my every expectation.'

'I know you never dreamt until I came along that you might enjoy three rug rats round your feet,' Emmie teased fondly, watching approvingly as she saw Zahir pull Saffy close with the quiet assurance of a firmly bonded couple. Emmie had never dreamt that falling in love could give her so much happiness.

'The more the merrier,' Bastian quipped, stunning dark golden eyes welded with sensual intent to her blushing face. 'We could head back into the house to check the catering arrangements.'

Her lovely face heated even more in the sunlight, hunger stirring as she looked up at him, a hunger laced with an excitement that had yet to fade. 'Whatever you like,' she told him breathily.

'Oh, I like...I like you very much,' Bastian growled raggedly, his arm tightening round her as he walked her back off the beach.

Her husband's desire for her never failed to make Emmie feel like the most exciting woman alive and she no longer remembered what it felt like to feel second best. She smiled, full of love and lust, happy and relaxed and grateful for the security and continuity of her tight-knit family circle.

* * * * *

COMING NEXT MONTH from Harlequin Presents®

AVAILABLE AUGUST 20, 2013

#3169 CHALLENGING DANTE
A Bride for a Billionaire
Lynne Graham

Dante Leonetti is convinced Topaz Marshall is after his family's money, and he's determined to seduce the truth from her lips. After experiencing Leonetti's ferocious reputation firsthand, will she be able to resist his legendary charms?

#3170 A WHISPER OF DISGRACE
Sicily's Corretti Dynasty
Sharon Kendrick

Rosa Corretti spent one unguarded night with Kulal and now this demanding sheikh wants to control her. The more Rosa resists, the stronger Kulal's desire. But will the arrogant sheikh accept this Corretti for more than one night?

#3171 LOST TO THE DESERT WARRIOR
Sarah Morgan

Desperate to escape an arranged marriage, Layla, Princess of Tazkhan, throws herself at the mercy of Sheikh Raz Al Zahki—her family's greatest enemy! But protection has a price.... This brooding desert king is determined to make her his queen.

#3172 NEVER SAY NO TO A CAFFARELLI
Those Scandalous Caffarellis
Melanie Milburne

Poppy Silverton's home, livelihood *and* innocence are under threat from playboy billionaire Rafe Caffarelli. Poppy will fight Rafe—and her attraction to him—all the way...and be the first woman to say no to a Caffarelli!

HPCNM0813RA

#3173 HIS RING IS NOT ENOUGH
Maisey Yates

Ajax Kouros has a plan—and being jilted at the altar is *not* part of it. His company's future depends on marrying a Holt, so when his bride's sister steps up to the altar...can he say no?

#3174 CAPTIVATED BY HER INNOCENCE
Kim Lawrence

Cesare Urquart can't possibly believe any worse of Anna Henderson. But when she arrives at his sprawling Scottish estate, Cesare gets a rush of adrenaline he hasn't felt for years and soon questions every notion he's had about her....

#3175 HIS UNEXPECTED LEGACY
The Bond of Brothers
Chantelle Shaw

Sergio Castellano will do whatever it takes to keep the heir he didn't know he had. But the longer he spends with ex-lover Kristen Russell the more he realizes the cracks she once made in his armor are still there.

#3176 A REPUTATION TO UPHOLD
Victoria Parker

When wild and shameless designer Eva St. George is caught with tycoon Dante Vitale it's guaranteed to cause a headline-worthy scandal. But if they can convince the world they're truly in love they might just both get what they want....

HPCNM0813RB